"I must settle fo..."

"I have always hoped that one day I would meet a woman I would want to love and live with the rest of my life, but it seems she has eluded me." The professor paused to look at Araminta, sitting very much at ease, smiling a little.

"Why are you telling me this?"

"I considered it right to explain my feelings before I ask you to marry me, Araminta."

Dear Reader,

Welcome to the latest book in our **Holding Out for a Hero** series. Every month for a whole year we'll be bringing you some of the world's most eligible men. They're handsome, they're charming but, best of all, they're single! And, as twelve lucky women are about to discover, it's not finding Mr. Right that's the problem—it's holding on to him!

Hold out for Harlequin Romance's heroes in coming months. Look out in August for:

Kit and the Cowboy
by Rebecca Winters

Award-winning author Becky has been called "The first Lady of Utah Romance novels..." *(Affaire de Coeur)*, and has recently been declared Utah Writer of the Year 1995, winning the Isolde Carlsen Award of Excellence.

Happy reading!

The Editors,
Harlequin Romance

Some men are worth waiting for!

The Bachelor's Wedding
Betty Neels

Harlequin Books

TORONTO • NEW YORK • LONDON
AMSTERDAM • PARIS • SYDNEY • HAMBURG
STOCKHOLM • ATHENS • TOKYO • MILAN
MADRID • WARSAW • BUDAPEST • AUCKLAND

ISBN 0-373-03415-6

THE BACHELOR'S WEDDING

First North American Publication 1996.

Copyright © 1995 by Betty Neels.

This edition published by arrangement with Harlequin Books S.A.

Printed in U.S.A.

CHAPTER ONE

THE pale February sunshine shining through the window highlighted the pleasant room beyond: a room of restful colours, greens and blues and greys, chosen no doubt to dispel the unease of the patients who entered it. Such a one was on the point of leaving, escorted to the door by Professor Jason Lister, a large, very tall man, remarkably handsome with it. He shook hands now, gave the lady a reassuring smile, and handed her over to his receptionist before closing the door again and going back to his desk to pick up his pen and begin to write.

He had hardly done so when the door opened and the receptionist poked her head round it. The professor didn't lift his head. 'Later, Mrs Wells, I'm due at the hospital in half an hour...'

'Yes, I know, sir, but it's Mrs Gault on the outside line. She says she must speak to you at once.'

He took off his reading-glasses and sighed. 'Very well.' He smiled as he spoke, and Mrs Wells, a middle-aged widow with a sentimental heart, beamed at him.

The voice at the other end of the phone was urgent and agitated. 'Jason? Is that you?' The voice didn't wait for an answer. 'I've just had a phone call from that place in Chile where Tom is—he's ill, and they want me to go there as soon as possible. I'm packing now. The children have half-term tomorrow and my flight goes mid-morning. I can't leave them here alone...'

'Where is Patty?'

'She's gone home to nurse her mother—I've been managing without her. Jason, what shall I do?'

'The children can come here; I'll find someone to collect them and look after them while you're away. I can't get to your place, I'm afraid, but I'll arrange something and phone you back. Don't worry more than you must.'

He put down the receiver, switched on the intercom, and asked Mrs Wells to come in.

'We have a problem,' he told her, his placid voice giving no hint of the size of it. And when he had finished telling her, he asked, 'Do you know of an agency where I can get someone at a moment's notice?'

'Yes, I do, sir. There's a very good one—in Kingsway, I believe. I can look it up. Will you speak to them?'

'Please, and as soon as possible.'

The mellifluous voice at the agency assured him that a person suitable to his requirements would be sent immediately.

'After six o'clock,' he made the request, 'and this is the address. It must be someone who is prepared to travel down to Tisbury—that is a small town in Wiltshire—by the early-morning train.'

The professor put down the receiver, put his spectacles on again and resumed his writing, and presently took himself off to the hospital in his dark grey Rolls Royce.

When the phone rang, Araminta was peeling potatoes. She dried her hands and went to answer it, although her sister Alice was sitting within a foot of the instrument, but then Alice had been told two years ago that she had anaemia and must lead a quiet life, an instruction which she obeyed to the letter, encouraged by their father, who doted on her.

'Yes?' said Araminta, anxious to get back to the potatoes.

'Miss Smith? I have an urgent job for you. Short-term, I believe.'

The woman from the agency gave the details in a businesslike manner. 'After six o'clock, and Professor Lister is depending on you.'

She rang off prudently before Araminta could refuse to go.

'That's a job,' said Araminta. 'I'll finish the potatoes, but perhaps you could cook the supper. I may be gone for a few hours.'

Alice looked alarmed. 'But, Araminta, you know I'm supposed to take life easily...'

'I don't suppose it would harm you to grill the chops, love. We do need the money—Father borrowed the housekeeping. I don't know what for.'

Alice looked awkward. 'Well, I did mention that I needed another dressing-gown, and he bought me one.'

Araminta turned round at the door. She spoke cheerfully, for there was no point in voicing her hurt that their father loved Alice dearly and regarded herself as the housekeeper and occasional wage-earner. He was kind to her and sometimes, when he remembered, he told her how useful it was that she was so handy around the house, as well as getting the occasional job from the agency. 'There's plenty of food in the fridge if I'm not back in a day or two.'

She finished the potatoes, changed into her tweed jacket and skirt—suitable for the occasion, she hoped—made sure that her hair was neatly coiled and that her nose was powdered, found an umbrella and went to catch a bus.

It was a long bus ride from her home in a narrow street near Warren Street station to the address she had been given—a small street close to Cavendish Square—and it was already after five o'clock. Six o'clock had long since struck by the time she reached the house, one of a terrace of Regency houses, pristine in their gleaming paint and shining brasswork, and she paused a moment to take a good look before mounting the steps to its front door.

It was opened by an elderly, rotund man with a fringe of hair and an impassive face. When she stated her name he stood aside for her to go in, waved her to a chair in the hall, and begged her to wait.

It was a pleasant hall, not large but welcoming, with crimson wallpaper, a polished wood floor and ormolu wall-lights; there were no pictures on the walls, but on the small mahogany table there was a beautiful bowl full of early spring flowers. Araminta sniffed appreciatively.

She wasn't kept waiting; the rotund man came back within a few minutes and asked her to follow him to the end of the hall and through a door at its end. The room had a large bay window, its heavy velvet curtains not drawn; there would be a garden beyond, she supposed, as she crossed the carpeted floor to stand before the large desk in one corner of the room. The professor got slowly to his feet, the book he had been reading in his hand, a finger marking the page. He stood for a moment, looking at her over his spectacles.

'Miss Smith? Miss Araminta Smith?'

She took exception to the lifted eyebrow. 'Yes—Araminta because it makes up for Smith, if you see what I mean!'

He perceived that this rather dowdy girl with no looks worth mentioning might not be quite what she seemed. He put his book on the desk reluctantly—for he had been relaxing with the poems of Horace—in the original Latin, of course.

'Please sit down, Miss Smith. I was expecting someone of a rather more mature... That is, your charges are young teenagers and, if you will forgive me for saying so, you look—er—rather young yourself.'

'Twenty-three,' said Araminta matter-of-factly. 'Young enough to be able to understand them and old enough to be listened to.' Since he looked doubtful, she added kindly, 'Try me—if I don't do you can find someone else, but the agency said that you needed someone urgently, so perhaps I could be of help until you do.'

She wasn't suitable but she would have to do, at least for the moment.

'It will be necessary for you to catch an early-morning train from Paddington. My nephew and niece are to stay here with me while their mother goes to her husband, who is ill. I have a manservant and his wife who live in the house, but they are too elderly to cope with teenagers. That will be your task.'

'For how long, Mr Lister?' She paused. 'Should I have said Doctor? The agency said you were in the medical profession.'

'Professor will do.' He smiled at her. She was nothing to look at, but he liked her sensible manner. 'Only for their half-term—a week. My sister has a splendid housekeeper, who has unfortunately gone to her home to nurse her mother. She should be back, and probably my sister will have returned by then.'

Everything quite satisfactory, thought Araminta; the problem of making arrangements for Alice and her father at a few hours' notice would be dealt with presently. She bade the professor a staid goodbye, and he called her back as she reached the door.

'You will need some money for fares and expenses,' he pointed out mildly, and took out his notecase. The amount he gave her was over-generous, and she said so.

'I shall expect an exact account of what you have spent,' he told her.

She flashed him a look from her dark eyes. 'Naturally,' she told him coldly.

He ignored the coldness. 'Mrs Buller will have everything ready; perhaps you will phone her as to what time you expect to arrive here. My sister has the number.'

Araminta nodded her tidy head. 'Very well, Professor Lister. Good evening.' He had opened the door for her, and she went past him into the hall and found Buller there, ready to speed her on her way. He gave her a fatherly smile.

'Quite an upheaval, Miss—the professor leads a very quiet life—but I daresay we shall manage.'

She hoped so, and then concentrated on her own problems.

It was to be expected that Alice would be difficult. Araminta had been working for the agency for some time now, but always on a daily basis; now she was actually going to leave Alice and her father on their own.

'How am I supposed to manage?' stormed Alice when Araminta arrived at home. 'You know how delicate I am—the doctor said I had to lead a quiet life. You're selfish, Araminta, going off like this. You must say you can't go.' She lapsed into easy tears. 'You might think of me...'

'Well, I am,' said Araminta sensibly. 'There's almost no money in the house, there's the gas bill waiting to be paid and the TV licence, and Father's salary won't be paid into the bank for another week. If you want to eat, I'll have to take this job. There's plenty in the fridge, and you can go to the shops for anything you need. I dare say a little walk would do you good. Or Father can shop on his way home.'

'Who is to make the beds and cook and do the housework?' wailed Alice.

'Well, I expect you could manage between you for a few days.'

'You're hard,' cried Alice. 'All you do is think of yourself.'

Araminta bit back the words on the tip of her tongue. She was, after all, a normal girl, wishing for pretty clothes and money in her pocket and a man to love her, and she saw no hope of getting any of these wishes. She went upstairs to her small bedroom in the little terraced house and packed a bag. Her wardrobe was meagre; she folded a sober grey dress—half-price in the sales and useful for her kind of job—a couple of sweaters, blouses and undies, dressing-gown and slippers, a tweed skirt and a rainproof jacket. Almost all she had, actually, and as she packed she could hear her father and sister talking in the sitting-room downstairs. She sighed a little, and made sure that she had all she needed in her handbag before going to join them.

It took the rest of that evening convincing her father that she really had to go. He was an easygoing man, spending money when he had it and borrowing when he hadn't, but even he had to admit that there was a shortage of cash in the house.

'Well,' he said easily, 'you go along and enjoy yourself, my dear. Alice and I will manage somehow. I'll use what money there is, for you'll bring your fees back with you, I suppose?' He smiled at her with vague affection. 'Our little wage-earner.' He got up. 'I'll make a pot of tea before we go to bed.'

'Not all the fees, Father,' said Araminta in a quiet voice. 'I need a new pair of shoes...'

She was up and dressed and eating a hasty breakfast when Alice came yawning into the kitchen. 'You might have brought me a cup,' she said plaintively.

'No time,' said Araminta, her mouth full. 'I'll phone you in a day or two when I know how things are going. Say goodbye to Father for me, will you?'

She dropped a kiss on her sister's cheek and flew out of the door with her case, intent on catching a bus to Paddington.

The train was half-empty and she sat in a window-seat, watching the wintry landscape, glad to have the next hour and a half to herself. She had few qualms about the job; she had been working for the agency for more than a year now, although this was the first time the job was expected to last as long as a week—perhaps not even that if Professor Lister found her unsatisfactory. She wasn't sure what to make of him; he hadn't approved of her, that was evident, but he had been pleasant enough in a rather absent-minded manner. Hopefully he would be out of the house for most of the day; she would only need to keep the children out of his way in the early mornings and the evenings.

When she got out of the train at Tisbury she was thankful to find an elderly taxi parked outside the station. The driver was pleasant and chatty and, when

she gave him the address, said at once, 'Oh, Mrs Gault—
poor lady. Worried sick, she is, with her husband ill on
the other side of the world. Come to give a hand, have
you? Half-term and all...'

The house was at the other end of the little town: a
red-brick dwelling in a large garden. There was nothing
elaborate about it; it was roomy, with large sash windows
and a handsome front door with a splendid fanlight—
what Araminta supposed one would describe as a
gentleman's residence. She paid the taxi-driver, took her
case and rang the bell, and then, since no one came,
banged the brass knocker.

The door was flung open then by a youngish woman
with untidy dark hair and Professor Lister's blue eyes.
'Oh, good, you're here. Do come in—you have no idea
how glad I am to see you.' She held out a firm, friendly
hand. 'I'm Lydia Gault...'

'Araminta Smith. What would you like me to do first?'

'You're heaven-sent, and sensible too. My taxi comes
for me in just two hours. I'm trying to get the children
organised—you've no idea... You'd like a cup of coffee,
I expect?'

Araminta put down her case and took off her coat.
She was wearing a tweed skirt and a blouse and car-
digan, and the sensible shoes which needed replacing.
'I'd love one. If you will show me where the kitchen is,
I'll make coffee for everyone, shall I? And, while we
drink it, you can tell me what you want me to do.'

'Through here—everything's in the cupboard in the
corner. I'll see how the children are getting on with their
packing. It's only for a week...'

Mrs Gault disappeared and Araminta put on the kettle,
found coffee, sugar and milk, assembled four mugs on
the kitchen table and opened a tin of biscuits, and when

that was done she got her notebook and pen from her handbag and laid them on the table too. She had a good memory, but she imagined that Mrs Gault would have a great many instructions to give her.

Mrs Gault came back again then, and the children with her. The boy, Jimmy, was tall and thin, with fair hair and a look of mischief about him; Gloria was younger, barely thirteen, but already very pretty. She was fair too, and she looked friendly. She was holding a large tabby cat in her arms and a Jack Russell trotted beside her, barking loudly.

She said at once, 'Tibs and Mutt are coming with us to Uncle Jason's.'

'Why not?' agreed Araminta, smiling. 'They couldn't possibly be left alone, could they?'

'He might mind,' said Jimmy.

'Well, if they are already there I don't suppose he'll object.' Araminta swallowed some coffee and picked up her pen. 'I assume there's a train this afternoon, Mrs Gault? We leave after you, I expect?'

'Yes, there's a train just after four o'clock. You'll need a taxi. Leave a note for the milkman, will you, and turn off the gas—I suppose we could leave the electricity on? Jimmy—what do you think?'

'Of course. Did you stop the papers? When is Patty coming back?'

His mother frowned. 'I phoned but there was no answer. Will you ring from Uncle Jason's?' She turned to Araminta. 'Will you leave the fridge and freezer on and be sure to lock up and see that all the windows are shut? Does Jason know what time you'll be back in London?'

'No, he asked me to ring his housekeeper as soon as I knew the train time.'

'Yes, of course. I'm sorry this is all such a muddle, but I suppose you're used to this kind of job.' Mrs Gault hesitated. 'I suppose you couldn't get some sort of meal for us all? Just anything,' she added vaguely. 'I've mislaid my sunglasses—I'm sure to need them. Gloria, finish your packing, darling, and, Jimmy, write a note for the milkman, will you?'

The three of them hurried away and Araminta, with Tibs and Mutt getting very much under her feet, flung open cupboards and fridge. Omelettes, oven chips and peas, she decided, since there wasn't time to cook anything elaborate. The animals needed to be fed too. She dealt with them first and, with them satisfied, set about getting the food ready.

She had the table in the kitchen laid after a fashion and the meal just ready when Mrs Gault and the children came back, and this time they were dressed ready to leave.

There was a great rush at the last minute: things missing, messages forgotten, and Mrs Gault, worried to death about her husband, hating to leave the children, spilling instructions until the final moment as she drove away in the taxi.

If Araminta had worked hard before Mrs Gault left, she found the rest of the afternoon even more arduous. Jimmy and Gloria were nice young people, but she was quick to see that they intended to reduce her to the level of a superior servant given half a chance. Only she didn't give them that; there was still a lot to do before they could leave. She toured the house with Jimmy, making sure that he watched her closing windows and locking doors before they all piled into the taxi.

The train was nearly empty. Mutt sat on Jimmy's knees and Tibby slept in her basket. The children didn't say much; now that the rush and bustle were over they were despondent, talking together quietly, ignoring her, and she for her part was glad to be left in peace, for she was tired now; her day had started early and was by no means over yet.

She had phoned the professor's house before they left Tisbury, and Buller had assured her that there would be an early supper and their rooms would be ready for them. 'Professor Lister will probably be late home, miss,' he had told her, and she hoped that that would be the case. She suspected that after a hard day's work at the hospital he relished his quiet evenings. It would be nice if she could get the children to bed before he returned.

It was quite a short journey from Paddington to his house, and Buller was waiting for them. The children treated him as an old friend and went at once to the kitchen to see Mrs Buller, leaving Araminta with the animals and the luggage. 'Now just you leave everything, miss,' said Buller kindly. 'There'll be a tray of tea in the sitting-room at the back of the hall in five minutes, and I'll get the bags upstairs. The children are on the right at the top of the stairs, miss, and your room is on the opposite side, if you care to go up.'

The stairs opened on to a square landing, with doors on either side and a passage leading to the back of the house. There was another smaller staircase too, but she didn't stop to look around her but opened the door Buller had pointed out and went in.

The room was fair-sized, light and airy and charmingly furnished, and there was a bathroom leading from it. She registered a strong desire to tumble on to the bed and go to sleep, but she took off her outdoor things, tidied her hair and did her face, and went downstairs again.

Buller was in the hall. 'Jimmy came for Tibs and Mutt,' he told her. 'Tea is ready for you, miss.'

She thanked him. 'Do you suppose the professor will mind about the animals?' she asked.

'I think not, miss. We have two dogs—golden Labradors. They are at present being exercised by Maisie, the housemaid. They are mild-tempered animals, however, and I foresee no trouble.'

He led the way to the small cosy room where he had set the tea-tray. There was a bright fire in the steel grate and comfortable chairs drawn up to it.

'I'll send the children to you, miss,' said Buller.

They came presently, not over-friendly. Araminta handed round tea and buttered toast, sandwiches and little cakes, and said in her sensible voice, 'When we've had tea, perhaps you would unpack your things and put them away? I don't know what arrangements are to be made about Tibs and Mutt—perhaps you've already seen to that?' She looked at Jimmy. 'Your Uncle has two dogs, I believe.'

'They'll be OK. They've met Mutt and Tibs when Uncle Jason has been down to see us.'

'Oh, good, and we can take Mutt for a walk—Hyde Park isn't far away, is it? And Tibs—will she settle down nicely?'

'She's my cat,' said Gloria. 'She sleeps on my bed.' She sounded sulky. 'Mrs Buller says we may have our supper in the kitchen; Uncle won't be home for ages. I'll unpack in the morning.'

'We'll go upstairs and unpack now,' said Araminta, 'otherwise you'll have to waste the morning doing it, when you might want to be doing something more interesting.'

'You're awfully bossy,' said Gloria. 'I suppose you'll eat in the kitchen with Buller and Mrs Buller and Maisie?'

'I dare say,' said Araminta equably. 'Never mind about me—let's get our things put away.'

'Patty always saw to our things for us,' grumbled Jimmy, tumbling shirts into the elegant little tallboy in his room.

Araminta turned to look at him from the pile of socks she was sorting out. 'Did she?' She sounded surprised. 'But you're almost grown-up, Jimmy.'

He muttered a reply, and she went to see how Gloria was getting on.

She was on the bed, leafing through a magazine, clothes strewn around on the chairs and the floor. She looked up as Araminta went in.

'I can't be bothered to put everything away—Patty always does it.'

'Well, Patty's not here, and since I'm not your nanny I think you had better tidy things up, for no one else is going to do it for you.'

'I don't think I'm going to like you,' said Gloria.

'That's a pity, but it's only for a few days, and if I make you unhappy I'm sure your uncle will try and get someone else from the agency. You see, there wasn't time for him to pick and choose—he had to take the only person free, and that was me.'

'Haven't you got a home?'

'Oh, yes, and a father and sister.'

'Why do you go out to work, then?'

Araminta said bracingly, 'Let's not talk about me. I'm not a bit interesting.'

She sat down on one of the little armchairs by the window and Gloria got off the bed and began to push things into cupboards and drawers.

'I'm tired,' she grumbled, but she sounded more friendly now. 'We had to get up ever so early.'

'Well, I expect supper won't be too long. Then you can come to bed with a book—your uncle's not here, so you don't need to stay up unless you want to.'

'Oh.' She glanced sideways at Araminta. 'Don't you mind Tibs sleeping on my bed?'

'Mind? Why should I mind? I like cats—dogs too. How old is she?'

'Daddy gave her to me on my sixth birthday.'

'She's very pretty, and your constant companion, I dare say.'

Gloria raked a comb through her hair. 'I want my supper.'

'Then let's go and see if it's ready.'

'Jimmy and me, not you,' said Gloria. 'The kitchen staff eat later.'

'We'd better get Jimmy,' said Araminta mildly. She was used, after a year at the agency, to living in a kind of no man's land while she was at a job. She had minded at first, but now she accepted whatever status was offered her.

Supper was ready, and Buller led the children down to the basement kitchen and then came back to where Araminta stood uncertainly in the hall.

'The professor telephoned. He hopes you will dine with him if you are not too tired. In the meantime, once Jimmy and Gloria are in bed, perhaps you would care to sit in the drawing-room? There are the day's papers there and some magazines.'

Araminta said bluntly, 'Aren't I supposed to take my meals in the kitchen?'

Buller said in a shocked voice, 'Certainly not, Miss. I have my instructions from the professor.'

'Well, thank you. I'll sit in the room where we had tea, shall I, until the children are ready? Will Professor Lister be very late, do you think?'

'There's no telling, miss. But I should imagine within the next hour or so.'

So she went and sat by the fire and thought about her day and contemplated the week ahead of her. Jimmy and Gloria were nice young people, she was sure, but, she suspected, spoilt. They were of an age to be rude and thoughtless—she could remember being both at their age—but as long as she could keep them occupied and happy, and at the same time out of their uncle's way unless he wished for their company, it shouldn't be too bad.

They joined her presently and, when she suggested that they might go to bed since they had had a long day, they demurred.

Araminta made no attempt to change their minds; instead she suggested that they might write letters to their mother. 'It takes nearly a week by airmail to get to that part of the world,' she told them, hoping that she was right. 'Your mother would be glad to hear from you both before she returns.'

'We'll phone her tomorrow,' said Jimmy.

'Even better,' said Araminta. 'You have the number?'

He gave her a sulky look. 'No, of course not. Uncle Jason will know.'

'Then you must be sure and get it from him before he leaves in the morning.'

She embarked on a tedious conversation about museums, some of which she suggested that they might go and see during the next few days. She was boring herself and, as she had intended, Jimmy and Gloria as well. It wasn't long before they declared that they would go to bed. Gloria scooped up Tibs, wished Araminta a sullen goodnight, and went upstairs, and Jimmy, after taking Mutt to the kitchen, followed her. Araminta glanced at the little carriage-clock on the mantelpiece. Almost nine o'clock and no sign of Professor Lister. Her insides rumbled emptily; she would have liked to go to bed too, but not on an empty stomach.

It was very quiet in the house. Buller had suggested that she should sit in the drawing-room once the children were in bed, so she got up and went to the door. The hall was empty and softly lighted and she went a little way into it, wondering which door led to the drawing-room. When she had come to see the professor she had been shown into a room at the back of the house, but there were doors on either side as well. She went to the nearest, opened it, and poked her head round. The dining-room, the oval table laid for dinner, presumably, the silver and glass gleaming in the light of the wall-sconces. She shut the door and crossed the hall to open the one opposite. The library, and a very handsome one too, and, although there was no one there, there was a bright fire burning, and a reading-lamp lighted on one of the small tables drawn up beside the comfortable chairs.

The professor's voice, soft in her ear, caused her to withdraw her head smartly. 'Finding your way around, I hope, Miss Smith?'

She turned to face him, breathing rather hard. 'You should never creep up on people,' she advised him. 'They might have weak hearts or something! Buller told me to sit in the drawing-room, if I would like that, but I haven't found it yet.'

He towered over her, looking concerned and at the same time impatient.

'My dear Miss Smith, my apologies—I trust no harm has been done to your heart or—er—something. The drawing-room is over here.' He led the way across the hall and opened another door, and she went past him and stood waiting.

'Please sit down. I dare say you're starving, but do have a glass of sherry before we dine.'

'Thank you. There's another thing, Professor Lister. Buller gave me a message that I was to dine with you, but if I might put you right about that... I'm just someone from an agency, not your guest. Usually I have my meals in the kitchen with the staff.'

'While you are in my house you will be so good as to take your meals with me and the children.'

He sounded annoyed, and she murmured, 'Very well, Professor,' in a placatory voice which he ignored.

'They are here, I presume?'

'Yes, there were no difficulties. They are upstairs in their rooms, but I can't say they are asleep because I don't know.'

'Difficult, were they?' he wanted to know. 'Nice children, but spoilt. My sister got away on time? She's not much good at organising things.'

'I believe that everything went well. There's just one thing—Jimmy has brought his dog with him and Gloria has her cat.' She peeped at him to see how he was taking the news, but his face was impassive. 'Your two dogs were out with the housemaid when we arrived, and she took them straight to the kitchen. I think they are still there, and so is Mutt—the Jack Russell.'

'Yes, Buller told me when I phoned. You like dogs?'

'Yes, I do.'

'Good—they can join us then. They appear to have absorbed Jimmy's dog. They are very good-natured beasts.'

He glanced up as Buller came in. 'Dinner, Buller? Good—and let Goldie and Neptune out, will you?'

They were crossing the hall when the dogs came padding to meet them. They gave muffled barks as he greeted them, and then went to Araminta, looking up at her with liquid brown eyes, ready to be friends. She crouched down, the better to greet them, while their master stood patiently. She looked up, smiling, and saw the look on his face—impatience? Indifference? She wasn't sure which of the two, but she got to her feet at once, feeling vaguely foolish. He must find her and the children a tiresome hindrance in his busy life.

'You must wish me at Jericho,' she said, and instantly wished the words unsaid.

'My dear young lady, on the contrary. Much as I have an affection for my nephew and niece, the thought of overseeing their daily activities fills me with alarm. You are more than welcome in my house.'

He was smiling and his voice was kind, but she had the feeling that he was thinking about something else.

She was hungry and the food was delicious. Mrs Buller must be a cordon bleu cook: the parsnip soup with just a hint of garlic, the roast pheasant, followed by a treacle tart which melted in the mouth, were witnesses to that. Araminta, quite famished by now, did full justice to the lot, but when the professor suggested that they might have their coffee at the table, she excused herself on the grounds of tiredness. She bade him a cheerful goodnight and wished that she hadn't seen the quick look of relief on his face; she was aware that she had hardly added to his evening's enjoyment.

CHAPTER TWO

ARAMINTA slept soundly. She was far too sensible to lie awake and speculate about the following day. No doubt it would have its problems, more easily faced after a good night's sleep. Waking up to find a cheerful young woman with a tea-tray and the information that breakfast was in half an hour was a splendid start to it.

The knowledge that their uncle was at home and expecting to see them at breakfast got Jimmy and Gloria out of bed, dressed and downstairs, without any coaxing on Araminta's part.

He was already at the breakfast-table and he looked up from reading his post to wish them good morning, but as Araminta came into the room behind them he got out of his chair, enquired politely if she had slept well, and invited her to take a seat at the table.

It was Gloria who asked, 'Oh, is Araminta going to have her meals with us?'

He offered Araminta a dish of scrambled eggs. 'Naturally Miss Smith will do so—why do you ask, Gloria?' His glance was frosty. 'She has sole charge of both of you while you are here, and be good enough to remember that. I am delighted to have you here, but you will have to fit into my household. Mutt is in the garden with Goldie and Neptune. Jimmy, you will make yourself responsible for him, won't you? And you, Gloria, will do everything necessary for Tibs. She should be safe enough in the garden as long as you are with her. You will be going out this morning, I dare say?' He glanced at Araminta, who nodded. 'Will you take all three dogs with you? The park is only a short walk away. I should be home about five o'clock. We might take the dogs in the car up to Hampstead Heath and give them a good run. Miss Smith will be glad of an hour to herself, I have no doubt.'

He gathered up his post. 'I'll give myself a day off on Saturday,' he told them. 'Decide what you want to do and let me know.'

The pair of them munched in silence after he had gone, then Jimmy said, 'We're quite old enough to look after ourselves . . .'

'Well, of course you are,' said Araminta briskly, 'but perhaps as you are your uncle's guests it would be polite to do as he asks. When we've had breakfast I'll go and ask Mrs Buller what time she serves lunch, while you two see to Mutt and Tibs.'

They muttered an answer and she finished her breakfast without haste, talking cheerfully about this and that, ignoring their unfriendly faces, and presently went down to the kitchen, introduced herself to Mrs Buller and sat down at the kitchen table at that lady's request so that they might discuss the days ahead.

'Professor Lister don't come 'ome for 'is lunch, miss, just now and then, like.' Mrs Buller beamed at her and Araminta beamed back at the cosy little woman. 'Suppose we say one o'clock sharp and tea at four o'clock? Dinner's at half-past seven when 'e's 'ome— leastways when 'e isn't called away. 'E entertains off and on, you might say, got a lot of friends but no one in particular, if you get my meaning—not a ladies' man, more's the pity. 'E'd make a fine husband. Likes 'is books . . .' Mrs Buller shook her grey head. 'Now, as to lunch, 'ow about a nice cheese soufflé? And the children will want chips and I'll do some baby carrots and a chocolate pudding...'

'That sounds lovely. I hope we aren't giving you a lot of extra trouble, Mrs Buller.'

'Bless you, miss, of course not.'

'I'll let Buller know when we go out and where we are going, shall I?'

'Now that sounds like good sense, miss.'

The morning went rather better than she had expected; the three of them went to the park with the dogs as she had suggested and, although Gloria and Jimmy made no effort to be friendly, at least they fell in with her carefully worded suggestions, couched in a friendly no-nonsense voice. They gave the dogs a good run and got back with just enough time to tidy themselves for lunch. Over the chocolate pudding Araminta broached her suggestion for the afternoon. 'I don't know this part of London very well,' she observed casually. 'I wondered if we got on a bus and went somewhere—another park, perhaps? We could look around and have a cup of tea, and then bus back in time for your uncle's return.'

The idea went down well, but they weren't going to let her have it all her own way.

'I'd rather go to Richmond,' said Jimmy.

'Why not? Would you like to take Mutt?'

He gave her a surprised look and she said calmly, 'Well, he's small enough to be carried if he gets tired, isn't he? Perhaps Tibs ought to have a few minutes in the garden before we go. I'll go and tell Buller—I don't expect Goldie and Neptune will need to go out again until we get back.'

The afternoon was a success; they sat overlooking the river, admired the Thames and the country beyond, and found a tea-room before getting a bus back. It had been an expensive outing, reflected Araminta, sitting on her bed counting the change in her purse, but worth every penny. Any minute now the professor would be home, and he would take the children and the dogs on the promised trip to Hampstead Heath...

When she went downstairs he was at home, sitting in his chair by the fire with his dogs at his feet. He got up as she went in, and she said quickly, 'Oh, you're home,' and blushed because it had been a silly thing to say. 'The children will be down in a few minutes; they're tidying themselves for the evening.'

'Sit down, Miss Smith. No difficulties?'

'None, thank you, Professor.'

The children came then, and she sat quietly while they recounted their day to him. 'But we're still going out with you, aren't we, Uncle?' asked Gloria.

'Of course. I'm glad you enjoyed yourselves. Go and get your coats; we'll go now.' When they had gone he said, 'Let me know how much you paid out on my behalf, Miss Smith,' and when she murmured vaguely, he said, 'Now if you please.'

So she told him. 'It's rather a lot of money, but they did enjoy their tea.'

'A small price to pay for their enjoyment. Have they seemed worried about their mother and father?'

'They haven't said anything to me, but I wouldn't expect them to...'

The children came back then. 'Isn't Araminta coming with us?' asked Gloria.

'No—I believe Miss Smith may be glad of an hour or so to herself.' He smiled kindly at her and she gave a grateful murmur. She wished that he would stop calling her Miss Smith, it highlighted her mousy dullness.

*   *   *

Day followed day, and Gloria and Jimmy showed no sign of liking her any better. True, they did what she asked them to do, fell in with her suggestions as to how to spend their days and treated her with politeness at any meal when their uncle was present. They had, for some reason, made up their minds not to like her, and in a way she could understand that; she was a stranger, wished on them at a moment's notice and instantly to be forgotten the moment they returned home to their mother's and Patty's casual spoiling.

It was towards the end of the week when Professor Lister received a phone call from his sister. She had no idea when she would be coming home; her husband was still very ill and it was impossible for her to leave him. 'I know how awkward it is for you to have the children,' she told him. 'Send them back in time for school—Patty should be back by now; she can look after them. That girl—what's her name?—Araminta can take them back and hand them over.'

'Don't worry about them,' he told her, 'I'll see that they get back home and settled in with Patty. I'm sorry Tom is still not fit, but stay as long as you need to—I'll drive down whenever I can and keep an eye on the children.'

'Bless you.' Lydia Gault rang off and he put the phone down and went to sit in his armchair. He would have to make time to drive the children back on Saturday and Araminta Smith would have to go with them. He could bring her back that same day and she could return home...

He got up presently and went to tell the three of them, who were playing a rather rowdy game of Monopoly in the sitting-room.

His news was received with mixed feelings by the children. They were troubled that their father was still ill and their mother wouldn't be coming home for a time; on the other hand they were pleased at the idea of going home again and returning to school and the loving care of Patty, who let them do exactly what they wanted. The professor watched their faces with a wry smile before he turned to Araminta.

'You will be kind enough to return with the children?' The question was a statement, politely put. 'I will drive you back in the evening.'

She agreed; she had telephoned Alice during the week and told her that she would be back at the weekend, listening patiently to the flood of complaints before putting the receiver down.

'I'll phone Patty,' said the professor. 'She's probably back by now—if not, I'll phone her at home.'

An urgent call from the hospital prevented him from doing that; it was only after his ward round that he remembered to do it. He pushed aside the notes he was writing in Theatre Sister's office and picked up the phone. There was no reply from his sister's home, but he had Patty's home number with him. He phoned that, waiting patiently while it rang.

Patty's soft Scottish voice said, 'Hello?'

He said at once, 'Patty? Jason Lister here. I don't suppose you've heard from Mrs Gault. She won't be able to return at present—Mr Gault isn't so well. I'll bring the children back on Saturday—so could you come back as soon as you can and open up the house? I know it's short notice, but perhaps you could take the night sleeper or fly back to Bristol or Exeter. Take a car, and don't spare the expense. I'll see to that——'

'Professor Lister, I can't—my mother's desperately ill. I cannot leave her—you must understand that—I was going to phone Mrs Gault when she got back. What is to be done?'

'Don't worry, Patty, we'll brush through. The young lady who has been looking after Jimmy and Gloria is still with us. I'll get her to go back with them and stay until either you or Mrs Gault get back. You stay and look after your mother.'

'You're sure, sir? I'll come the moment I can.'

'Stay as long as you need to,' he told her, 'and let me know how you get on.' He hung up; it was providential that Araminta Smith was still with them. He would see her as soon as he got home.

Which was late that evening. The children were in bed and Araminta was sitting uneasily in the drawing-room when he got back. She didn't much like sitting there on her own but Buller had told her that the professor wanted her to make use of the room whenever she wished. One more day, she was thinking, then back home to a disgruntled Alice and the careless affection of her father, eager to know how much she had earned. The money had been hard-earned too; true, she had lived in the lap of luxury in this lovely house, but not for one moment had the children shown her any sign of friendliness.

As for Professor Lister, he treated her with an impersonal politeness which held no more warmth than when they had first met.

She got to her feet as he came in, the dogs at his heels. Her 'Good evening, Professor Lister,' was quietly said. 'I was just going to bed. You must be tired...'

'Yes, but please don't go for a moment. I have something to say to you.'

She sat down again and he sat in his chair opposite to her. She looked at his tired face. 'You should go to your bed,' she told him in her matter-of-fact way, 'but perhaps you are hungry too. Shall I go and see if Mrs Buller could warm up some soup?'

'I believe Buller has the matter in hand, but it is kind of you to bother. Perhaps you will have a drink with me first?'

He got up and poured her a glass of sherry and gave himself some whisky. 'We have a problem,' he told her, 'and I must rely on you to solve it.'

She listened without interruption, and when he had finished she said simply, 'How very unfortunate. Of course I will do as you ask, only I must go home and get some clothes—I only brought enough for a week with me.'

'Certainly. I'll drive you home tomorrow—I should be home round about four o'clock. That will give you time to pack whatever you need to take there and decide what you wish to take with you. I have no idea how long you may need to stay, but I would suggest that you think in terms of two weeks.' He saw the doubt in her face. 'That presents difficulties? Your family?'

'My sister isn't very used to running the house.'

'She is alone?'

'No. No—but my father is away all day.' She would have stopped there but the faint enquiry in his face forced her to go on. 'She's delicate.'

He said kindly, 'Well, suppose we go to your home and see what she says; if necessary I could arrange for her to have some help. May I ask in what way your sister is delicate?'

'Well, the doctor told her she would have to take things easy.'

'This was recent, this advice?'

Araminta wrinkled her forehead in thought. 'Well, no—about two years ago.'

'Has she been taking things easy since then? Does she see her doctor regularly?'

'Not since then.' Araminta glanced at him as she said it, and surprised a look on his face; she wasn't sure what the look was because it had gone at once. She must have imagined it.

The children were upset, looking at her as though it were all her fault. She was thankful when the professor came home the next afternoon, his calm, logical acceptance of the situation allowing them to take a more cheerful view of it.

'I'll phone each evening,' he promised them, 'and if I can manage it I'll come down at the weekend, and as soon as I have any news I'll let you know. I know you both want to help your mother and father, and the best way of doing that is to give them no cause to worry about you. Will you get your things packed up while I take Miss Smith to her home to get what she needs? We'll go after breakfast tomorrow—that will give us time to do any shopping and air the house. When your mother and father are back home, I promise we'll all have a mar-vellous celebration.'

He had nothing to say as he drove Araminta home; he wasn't a talkative man and his well-ordered life had been turned upside-down and, even though the three of them would be gone, he would still need to keep an eye on them from a distance, and that over and above his own busy life.

The contrast between his handsome house and her own home was cruel, but she didn't allow it to bother her.

He stopped before its front door and she prepared to get out. She stopped halfway. 'I shall be about half an hour,' she told him. 'Would you like to come in, or perhaps you would rather come back?'

His mouth twitched. 'I'll come in, if I may.' It would be interesting to see how this unassuming girl, who had fitted into the quiet luxury of his home with unself-conscious naturalness, behaved in her own house. Besides, he had a wish to meet the delicate sister. As plain as her sister? he wondered.

Araminta put her key in the lock and opened the door, and stood aside to allow him to pass her into the narrow hall. It was a bit of a squeeze, for he was so very large, but she said nothing, only called softly, 'Alice? Alice, I'm back...'

Alice's voice came from the kitchen. 'And about time too, I'm sick of all this beastly housework...' Her voice got louder as she opened the door wider and came through, and then changed miraculously as she saw Professor Lister. 'Oh, we weren't expecting you...' Her cross face became wreathed in smiles.

'This is Professor Lister, Alice. My sister, Professor. Alice, I shall be away for another week or ten days. I've come to collect some more clothes. I've brought my case with me...'

The professor had shaken hands and smiled but not spoken; now he said, 'Ah, yes, I'll fetch it in for you.' And he went out to the car again.

Alice clutched Araminta's arm. 'Why didn't you warn me? I'd have had my hair done and put on a decent dress. He's quite something.' She added peevishly, 'The house is in a mess...'

'I doubt if he notices,' said Araminta prosaically. 'He's a bit absent-minded.'

Alice tossed her head. 'I'll make him notice me...' She turned to smile at him as he came back into the house. 'You run along, dear,' she said sweetly to Araminta. 'I daresay Professor Lister would like a cup of coffee.'

Araminta climbed the stairs to her room and set about the business of finding fresh clothes, stout shoes and an all-enveloping overall, since it seemed likely that she would be expected to do the housework as well as keep an eye on Jimmy and Gloria. That done, she took a pile of undies and blouses down to the kitchen, stuffed them into the washing-machine and switched it on. Alice wasn't likely to iron them, but at least they would be clean when she got back. She could hear voices in the sitting-room, and Alice's laugh, as she went back upstairs to collect her writing-case and choose a book to take with her. She thought that she might need soothing by bedtime each day, and ran her hand along the row of books by her bed. She chose *Vanity Fair* and Thackeray's *Ballads and Songs*. She hesitated, her small, nicely kept hand hovering over *Jane Eyre*, but there wasn't room for it in her case. She closed the case, carried it downstairs, and went into the sitting-room. The professor was sitting in one of the shabby armchairs by the fireplace and he got up as she went in. Alice was sitting on the old-fashioned sofa. She looked prettier than ever, thought Araminta without envy, but it was a pity that the room was so untidy, more than untidy, grubby. Why did Alice look so cross, anyway?

She looked quickly at the professor, but he looked as he always did, pleasant and at the same time unconcerned, as though his mind were elsewhere. She could hardly blame him for that; she longed to get a duster and tidy up a bit. All the same, Alice was surely pretty enough to override her surroundings—something must have gone wrong...

'I'm ready, Professor,' she said briskly. 'I'll let you know as soon as possible when I'll be coming home,' she told her sister, and was rewarded by a pouting face.

'I suppose I'll have to manage. Lucky you, it'll be as good as a holiday.'

Alice got up and offered a hand to Professor Lister, looking at him in a little-girl-lost manner which Araminta found irritating, although probably, being a man, he liked it. He showed no signs of either liking or disliking it; she had never met a man who concealed his feelings so completely.

'I'm sure you must be relieved to know that, after all this time, whatever it was your doctor diagnosed has apparently cured itself. I must urge you to go and have a check-up. It isn't for me to say, but I feel sure that you have little reason to fear for your health.' He shook her hand firmly and stood aside while Araminta kissed her sister's cheek, but Alice was still peevish. She went over to the door with them and wished them a cold goodbye as they got into the car, shutting the door before they had driven away.

Araminta peeped at her companion's profile; he looked stern.

'As I said it is, of course, not for me to say, but I believe that your sister is in excellent health. I suggested that she should see her doctor so that he might reassure her. If she had needed medical care when she first went to him he would have advised her to see him regularly.'

'He told her that she had to take things easily.'

'But not for two years or more.'

'It's very kind of you to concern yourself, Professor Lister,' said Araminta frostily, 'but perhaps...' She paused, not quite sure how to put it. 'You're a surgeon,' she pointed out.

'I am also a doctor of medicine,' he told her blandly. 'Have you all that you require for the next week or so?'

She wondered if she had been rude. 'Yes, thank you. I'm sorry if I was rude; I didn't mean to be.'

'It is of no consequence. Indeed, I prefer outspokenness to mealy-mouthed deception.'

They were almost back at his house. 'We shall leave directly after breakfast,' he observed, with the cool courtesy which she found so daunting. 'Will you see that the children are ready by nine o'clock—and the animals, of course?' He drew up before his door and got out and opened her door for her. 'I expect you would like an hour or so in which to pack for yourself—I'll take the children out with the dogs.'

He stood in the hall looking down at her, unsmiling, while Buller fetched her bag from the car. He must find all this a most frightful nuisance, she reflected, his days turned upside-down and, even if he's fond of the children, he doesn't like me overmuch. A sudden wish to be as pretty as Alice swam into her head; it was the impersonal indifference which she found so hard to bear.

She thanked him in her quiet way, and went upstairs and began to pack her things before going to see if Jimmy and Gloria had made a start on theirs. They hadn't, and it would be too late by the time they got back and had had dinner; getting them up in the morning would be bad enough. She fetched their cases and began to pack for them as well.

The professor went to his study after dinner and Araminta, mindful of his placid, 'We shall leave directly after breakfast. Will you see that the children are ready by nine o'clock,' finished the packing, persuaded the children to go to their beds and went to her room, intent on a long hot bath and washing her hair, but she had got no further than taking the pins out when there was a tap on the door. There was Buller with a request that she would go at once to the study as the professor had been called away and wished to see her before he went.

'He'll have to wait while I get my hair up,' said Araminta.

'If I might venture to say so, miss, the professor is anxious to be gone—an urgent matter at the hospital, I believe. Could you not tie it back or plait it?'

'Well, all right, I expect I'd better.' She began with quick fingers to weave a tidy rope of hair over one shoulder; it hung almost to her waist, thick and mousy, and she was braiding the last inch or so when Buller knocked on the study door and held it open for her.

The professor was stuffing papers into his bag. He looked up as she went in and, if he noticed the hair, he made no comment.

'Miss Smith, I have to return to the hospital, and I am not sure when I shall get back. There may not be time to discuss anything at our leisure before we leave. You will need money for household expenses—it is in this envelope, together with the telephone numbers you might need in an emergency. You will not hesitate to get in touch with me should you judge it necessary, or if you need more money. Does the agency pay you?'

'Yes, when I've finished the job.'

'You have enough money for yourself?'

She had very little, but she wasn't going to say so. 'Quite enough, thank you, Professor Lister.' She had spoken quickly and he gazed at her sharply. He didn't say anything, though, only nodded and gave her the envelope. 'I'll keep an account of what I spend,' she assured him.

'If you wish to do so.' He sounded uninterested. 'I'll see you in the morning. Breakfast at eight o'clock.' He went to open the door for her and, as she went past, he said softly, 'I like the hair. Why do you bundle it up out of sight?'

Araminta was annoyed to find herself blushing. 'It gets in the way,' she said and added, for no reason at all, 'I was going to wash it.'

She slid past him and away across the hall and up the staircase; halfway up she remembered that she hadn't wished him goodnight.

By some miracle Araminta managed to get the children and the animals ready and down to breakfast by eight o'clock. There was no sign of their uncle, and Jimmy was quick to point out that she need not have chivvied them into such haste, but he had scarcely finished his grumbling when Professor Lister came in. He was wearing casual clothes and greeted them in his usual manner, but he looked tired, and Araminta wondered if he had been up half the night. She had the good sense not to ask, though, but ate her breakfast, saw to it that Jimmy and Gloria ate theirs, and then excused the three of them so that the animals could have last-minute attention. Obedient to his wish, she presented her small party at nine o'clock precisely in the hall. The cases had already been brought down and Buller had put them in the boot. Goldie and Neptune were there too, and the professor began to load the Rolls with its passengers.

'You will sit in front with me, Miss Smith,' he observed. 'If you will have Tibs and his basket on your knee, Mutt can sit on Jimmy, and Goldie and Neptune can sit on the floor.'

If they felt rebellious the children didn't say so, but got into the car and settled down with room to spare, leaving Araminta to settle herself in the comfort of the front seat.

Beyond enquiring as to everyone's comfort, the professor had little to say, and Araminta, guessing that he was tired, kept silent. The children sounded happy enough and the animals were giving no trouble; she sat back and allowed her thoughts to wander.

They didn't wander far. She was very conscious of the professor's vast silent bulk beside her; if he had a private life—friends, girlfriends, a woman he loved—there had been no sign of them during the week; as far as she had seen, his days were wholly occupied by his work. He must have a private life, she thought. I dare say he's tucked it out of sight while we've been living in his house. She began to think about the kind of woman he might love. Beautiful, of course, exquisitely dressed, amusing and witty, knowing just how to soothe him when he got home from a busy day at the hospital...

She looked out of her window and saw that they were well away from London; the A303 wasn't far off. He wasn't wasting time.

She turned to see if everything was as it should be on the back seat and, since it was, settled back again.

'Comfortable?' asked the professor.

'Yes, thank you. Have you been up all night?'

He laughed a little. 'Am I driving so badly? Not all night; I got home just after two o'clock.'

'You would have time for a nap before you have to return.'

'I'm flattered by your concern, Miss Smith, but I am quite rested.'

Snubbed, thought Araminta, and looked out of the window again.

Halfway down the A303 he stopped at a Happy Eater, and everyone piled out except Tibs, asleep in her basket. The dogs on their leads were walked by Jimmy and his uncle while Araminta and Gloria went inside, in a hurry to get to the ladies', and then to find a table. They were joined shortly by Jimmy and the professor, who ordered coffee for all of them and a plate of buns. The coffee was hot and the children wolfed the buns as though they were starving, but no one wasted time in casual talk. In ten minutes they were back in the car and on their way. Tisbury wasn't far; Professor Lister took a left-hand turning into a side road and they were at once surrounded by rural Wiltshire. There was only one village on their way, Chilmark, then they were back running between high hedges and scattered farms. Araminta gave an appreciative sniff and the professor observed, 'Restful, isn't it? When we arrive I shall leave you to open up the house, make the beds and so on. I'll take the children into the village—you'll need bread and milk and so on, won't you?'

'Yes, do you want a list? I can take a quick look in the fridge and the freezer.'

'That would help. Do you feel up to cooking a meal?'

'Yes, of course.'

They lapsed into silence, but this time it seemed to her that the silence was friendly.

The children were glad to be home. They rushed inside as soon as the professor had unlocked the door and then, at his placid request, carried the bags indoors and upstairs. That done, he said, 'If you'll see to Tibs, Gloria,

Jimmy can see to the dogs while Miss Smith and I make a list of the food we'll need. We'll go down to the village and do the shopping while she gets the place aired.'

Whatever made me think that he was absent-minded? reflected Araminta, busily writing a list of the food to be bought.

Once they were out of the house, leaving her with Tibs for company, she set about opening the windows, looking into the cupboards and peering into drawers. The linen-cupboard was nicely filled; she took the bedlinen off the beds and filled the washing-machine. The beds could be made up later. She laid the table for lunch, peeled the potatoes she found in the garden shed, and nipped round with a duster—not ideal, but all she had time for.

They came back laden. 'Sausages,' said the professor, emptying plastic bags all over the table, 'spring greens, carrots and turnips. Apples, oranges and lettuces. Jimmy has the rest and Gloria went to the baker's. We'll go into the garden while you get the lunch—do you want a hand?'

'No, thanks.' She glanced at the clock. 'Half an hour?'

All the same he stowed away the butter, milk and cheese before he went into the garden, the dogs trailing after him.

Araminta was a good cook: the sausages, grilled to a golden brown, lay on a mound of creamed potatoes, she had glazed the carrots with sugar and butter, and the spring greens, chopped fine, added a note of colour. Everything was eaten, as were the cheese and biscuits which followed. A pot of coffee washed everything down nicely and the professor sat back with a sigh.

'A delicious meal, Miss Smith,' he observed. 'We'll wash up while you do whatever you want to do. Gloria, don't forget to feed that cat of yours, and what about the dogs?'

Araminta left them to it, and sped upstairs to make beds, put out towels and tidy the rooms. There would be several loads of washing, but she could iron all day, if necessary, when the children had gone back to school.

When she got back to the kitchen everything had been tidily put away and she found the three of them in the hall by the open door.

'There you are,' said Professor Lister. 'I'm going back now—I'll phone you this evening and, if you need help or advice, don't hesitate to ring me. I'll do my best to come down.'

He nodded to her, said goodbye to Jimmy and Gloria, got into his car with the dogs and drove away. The three of them stood watching the car disappearing down the drive and into the lane, and even when it was out of sight they still stood there.

It was Araminta who said briskly, 'I expect you've heaps of things you want to do, but first will you let me have all your washing? I dare say there are some things you'll need for school on Monday.'

'Patty usually...' began Gloria, and thought better of it. 'All right, but then I want to go and see Jean down at the Rectory.'

'Why not?' agreed Araminta cheerfully. 'But please both be here for tea. Half-past four. We can discuss supper then.'

She was surprised that they didn't demur, but fetched their washing, put Mutt on his lead, and went off together—which gave her time to check the cupboards again, pick some flowers from the garden and unpack her own things; all the while, Professor Lister was never far from her thoughts.

CHAPTER THREE

ARAMINTA went to bed that night thankful that the day had gone so well. The children had returned for their tea and afterwards had helped her wash up, albeit grudgingly. They were still unfriendly but at least they did what she asked them to do with only a modicum of grumbling. The professor had telephoned as he had promised, a brief conversation undertaken against a background of voices—women's voices as well as men's. Probably he was relaxing with his friends; she pictured him in his lovely house, entertaining them. A mistake, of course. He was in Theatre Sister's office, drinking coffee after operating...

At breakfast the next morning Jimmy said reluctantly, 'Uncle Jason said we were to take you to church with us.'

'Why, thank you, Jimmy, I shall be glad to go. The morning service?'

'Yes—who's going to cook our dinner?'

'I shall. It can cook in the oven while we are away. What do you do with Mutt?'

'Shut him in the house; he doesn't mind as long as Tibs is there too.'

So they went to church, and when they got back the steak and kidney pie she had made from the contents of the freezer the night before was nicely cooked. She left it warm in the oven while the potatoes and the greens cooked. They had brought a carton of ice-cream back with them on the previous day; she scooped it out into three dishes, embellished it with some chocolate sauce she had found, and put it back in the freezer. Everything was ready by the time the children had fed Mutt and Tibs.

They both ate everything she put before them, although they didn't say if they liked it, and once they had finished they told her that they were going over to a friend's house. 'We'll probably stay for tea,' said Gloria airily.

'Why not? But please tell me where you are going, in case I should want you rather urgently.' And at their blank stares she added gently, 'Your mother might telephone, or your uncle, and do give me a ring if you're staying for tea, will you? Do you want to take Mutt?'

'Of course, and I wish you wouldn't make a fuss,' said Jimmy rudely.

'Well, of course I could wash my hands of the pair of you,' observed Araminta cheerfully, 'but your uncle asked me to be here until someone gets back and I said that I would. We'll all have to make the best of it, won't we?' She began to gather up the plates. 'Write it on the pad over there, will you, and please put the phone number. Tea at half-past four, if you decide to come home.'

She was prepared for them to ignore her request, and it was an agreeable surprise when Gloria phoned to say that they *were* staying for tea and would be home in time for supper. It gave her a chance to sit down for a bit with a pot of tea and a plate of scones while she jotted down menus for the week ahead.

It was while she was getting the supper that she realised that there was a problem she hadn't thought of—Mrs Gault had driven the children to their schools each day and either she or Patty had fetched them back. There was a car in the garage but that wouldn't be of much use since she couldn't drive. There would be a school bus, of course, but probably that served the comprehensive school and the other state schools in Salisbury. Gloria was at a private girls' school a few miles from Tisbury, and Jimmy at a minor public school lying in the other direction. Not far in a car, but they could be at the North Pole if there was no transport. She sat and wrestled with the problem for some time, and reluctantly decided to wait until the children came back to see if between them they could think of a way out of their dilemma.

Hire a car? she wondered. But would Professor Lister agree to that? Perhaps she could phone him and ask his advice.

She had no need to do so, for he phoned within the next half-hour.

Her, 'Hello,' was breathless with relief.

He said at once, 'Problems? You sound quietly desperate.'

'I am.' She explained with commendable brevity.

'I should have thought of that. Leave it with me. My sister has several friends in the village. I believe the doctor's sons go to Jimmy's school—he can give him a lift and drop Gloria off on his way. I'm sure that he will help. I'll ring you back, so don't worry.' He rang off with a quick goodbye and she went back to her cooking. It was all very well to tell her not to worry, but she wouldn't feel easy until he phoned again.

Which he did, shortly before the children came home. 'Mrs Sloane—Dr Sloane's wife—will collect Jimmy and Gloria at eight o'clock and bring them back after school.'

Araminta thanked him. 'I'm sorry I had to bother you.'

He said coolly, 'It was merely a question of picking up the telephone, Miss Smith.' His goodbye sounded like an afterthought.

As they sat down to supper presently, Jimmy said, 'We shan't be able to go to school—Mother always took us in the car—or Patty. I don't suppose you can drive a car.'

'No, I can't. Mrs Sloane is calling for you both each day and will give you a lift back in the afternoon. Your uncle has arranged it.' She smiled at him. 'Eight o'clock at the gate, so we'd better have everything ready before you go to bed. Do you take anything with you? Lunch or a snack?'

Gloria said prissily, 'We don't go to state schools, Araminta.'

A remark Araminta let pass. 'What about Mutt and Tibs? Will you let me know if they have to be fed and when—and does Mutt go for a walk during the day?'

'If you take him on his lead, and he has a biscuit at lunchtime.'

'Tibs has a meal then too,' said Gloria. 'Of course, you don't belong here so she might run away—then it'll be your fault.'

Araminta reminded herself silently that this was a job and she was being paid for it. She said equably, 'Oh, I like cats, but if you don't like to leave her in my care perhaps we could find a good cattery where she would be safe.'

Jimmy frowned at his sister. 'Tibs will be OK—you're being a bit silly.'

'And rude,' added Araminta mildly.

They weren't an easy pair to handle; they loitered over their breakfast, had a last-minute hunt for school-books,

and their rooms, when she went upstairs to make the
beds, were in a state of chaos. 'Patty must be an angel,'
observed Araminta to Tibs, who was comfortably
snoozing on Gloria's bed. At least she had the house to
herself while she vacuumed and dusted, hung the washing
on the line at the bottom of the garden and gave the
kitchen a good clean. Jimmy had said something about
a Mrs Pretty, who came twice a week, but perhaps Mrs
Gault had told her not to come while she was away.
Araminta, armed with a shopping-basket and the
household purse and with Mutt on his lead, took herself
off to the village to buy lettuce, cucumber and tom-
atoes. The children wanted baked beans for their supper;
she intended to add bubble-and-squeak and a small salad.
As for their demands for Coca-Cola, she had different
ideas. Without conceit she knew that her home-made
lemonade was perfection itself. She added lemons to her
basket at the village stores and replied suitably to the
proprietor's questions. Mr Moody was stout and bald
and good-natured, and he liked a chat.

'A bit of a carry-on up at Mrs Gault's, eh? Poor lady,
and then that Patty going off at a moment's notice—
not that she could help that, poor soul.' He eyed
Araminta. 'You'm a young woman with your hands full,
I've no doubt. Need their dad, do Jimmy and Gloria.
Not but what Professor Lister don't do his best, and
him a busy man. Coming down this weekend, no doubt?'

'I don't know; I expect that will depend on whether
he can get away or not.'

Araminta smiled and Mr Moody decided that, plain
though she might be, she had a lovely smile.

'Well, just you let me know if there is aught I can do,'
he told her, 'and that'll be two pounds and sixty-three

pence.' He handed over the change. 'Half a mo'—that Mutt usually has a bit of biscuit...'

'There's a Mrs Pretty,' began Araminta, 'but the children weren't sure if Mrs Gault had told her she would be away.'

'Bless your heart, love, Mrs Gault didn't need to tell her. Everyone knows everyone else's business here. She was in the shop this morning early, and mentioned that she'd be going up as usual.'

'Oh, good. When is that?'

'Tomorrow and Friday mornings—half-past eight till noon. Does the rough.'

'Oh, good,' said Araminta again, and wished him a cheerful good day.

There was plenty to do when she got back: more washing to hang out, ironing to do, a meal to get for herself and then tea to lay, ready for the children's return. She made a cake and some scones, and boiled the potatoes ready for the bubble-and-squeak and, after her own lunch, set about making the lemonade. It was an old recipe, involving the steeping of the lemons in boiling water and the sieving of the fruit and the careful adding of sugar and finally, when it was nicely cool, a few sprigs of mint.

The children came racing into the house, calling for Tibs and Mutt, flinging down hat and cap and coats and demanding tea.

Araminta had come into the hall to meet them. She said in a firm voice, 'The kettle is boiling, and tea will be put on the table when you have picked your things off the floor and hung them up, changed your shoes and washed your hands.'

They stared at her. 'Patty always...' began Gloria, and thought better of it. She began to gather up her coat and hat, and after a moment Jimmy did the same. Under Araminta's eye they changed their shoes and washed their hands in the cloakroom and then went sulkily into the kitchen.

Araminta had taken pains with the tea; there were scones, split and buttered, strawberry jam, Marmite sandwiches and a fruitcake.

'You didn't make these, did you?' asked Jimmy, sitting down at the table.

'Yes. Now tell me, at what time do you have supper? After your homework and before bed?'

'We have supper when we feel like it,' Gloria said.

'Ah, I see—you get your own? That's all right, then.'

'Hold on,' said Jimmy, 'we can't cook—don't be stupid, Gloria.'

Araminta allowed them to bicker for a few minutes. Then she said, 'Homework after tea, then supper. That gives you time to do whatever you want before bed.'

'You're a tyrant—no, a martinet,' declared Gloria. 'We always do what we want.'

'So do I,' said Araminta calmly. 'Have another slice of cake?'

Much later that evening, when the professor phoned, she told him everything was fine. 'Jimmy and Gloria will be sorry to have missed you...'

'It's late—I'm sorry. I'll ring earlier tomorrow.'

'You have no news?' asked Araminta.

'None. I think you must be prepared to remain for at least ten days. Do you wish me to contact your father?'

'Thank you, but there is no need. I told Alice I'd be away for a week or longer.'

He rang off then, after bidding her a civil goodnight.

Life settled down into a rather uneasy pattern; the children were no friendlier, but at least they did what she asked of them; she suspected that the telephone conversations with their uncle each evening had something to do with that. He was punctilious in his daily phone call but it was brief, and her report was just as brief. Sometimes, she reflected wistfully, he sounded as unfriendly as his young relations.

There was Mrs Pretty to brighten things two days a week, a lady whose appearance had nothing to do with her name; she was a big bony woman, nudging sixty, with a craggy face and a disconcerting squint. She had a powerful voice, smoked like a chimney, and had an elaborate hair-do which was tinted an unsuitable chestnut with highlights. She had marched up to the house on Tuesday morning, announced who she was, declared that Araminta didn't look fit to cope with the Gault youngsters and said that she intended to turn out the kitchen, but not before she had had her usual cup of tea. 'And I like it strong,' she had added.

She was a treasure, going through the house like a whirlwind, cigarette dangling from her lip and, over the snack lunch she shared with Araminta, making her familiar with those who lived in the village. 'Not a bad lot,' she concluded, 'and Mrs Gault's well-liked, though them kids of hers need a firm hand. A good thing when their dad's back again. That Patty's a good sort, but she spoils them rotten. A pity that uncle of theirs can't have 'em for a while—nice gent—bit absent-minded, likes to bury his 'andsome 'ead in a book, don't seem to notice the girls much—'as a way with 'im, though. Like him, do you, my lovely?'

Araminta blinked. No one had ever called her 'my lovely' before; she found it delightful. 'Yes, I like him,' she agreed, 'although, of course, I don't know him at all well. The children are very fond of him.'

'Let's hope 'e gets down here a bit then, and knocks some manners into the pair of them. Need to go away to school they do—well, Jimmy will be boarding next term, going to some posh place.' Mrs Pretty swallowed the rest of her tea and took herself off to clean the bathroom the children used. 'It needs a fair walloping,' she shouted over a massive shoulder as she left the kitchen.

Well-primed on her second visit, Araminta had a pot of tea, strong enough to knock out an elephant, ready on the kitchen table. Mrs Pretty drank the pot dry, recommended that Araminta should get on with the ironing while she gave the drawing-room the once-over, and took herself off until it was time for elevenses.

'Coming for the weekend, is 'e?' she asked, and bit into one of Araminta's cakes. 'Nice little cook you be.'

'I don't know; he hasn't said so—he is a very busy man.'

Mrs Pretty shrugged. 'Doctors—well, he's a surgeon, isn't he? Don't hold with them meself. Old miseries, telling me that a cig's bad for me. Smoked all me life I 'ave, and look at me.'

Araminta hoped that she was looking at the right eye; it was difficult with the squint. 'I'm sure you're awfully fit,' she agreed politely, 'but I don't think smoking does much good...'

Mrs Pretty laughed; she had a loud, cheerful laugh. 'Me old granny always said, "A little of what you fancy does you good", and I fancy a cig off and on. Got a young man, have you, love?'

'No. I'm not pretty,' said Araminta, baldly and without self-pity.

'What's that got to do with it? Look at me, I'm no beauty.' Mrs Pretty let out another laugh. ''Ad two 'usbands. Beauty's but skin-deep, ducks, and don't you forget it.'

Which was all very well, reflected Araminta, but it hardly weighed against a pretty face.

It was Saturday and there had been no word from Mrs Gault or Patty. Araminta did her best to reassure Jimmy and Gloria, and wished that their uncle would at least telephone, something he hadn't done for the past two days. She had written home and warned her father that she might not be home for some days yet, but she had had no reply and she didn't want to phone because Alice would try to persuade her to return, something she didn't intend to do until she was no longer needed. It was a blessing that Gloria and Jimmy were asked out to tea in the village on Saturday; it helped the day along. She had suggested that they might like to show her something of the countryside around the village, but the idea had fallen flat and, since they so obviously didn't wish for her company, she busied herself around the house and about the garden. She hoped that they had plans of their own for Sunday, but she was too wise to ask.

It was a pity that they held her in such dislike, but she could understand that—in their eyes she wasn't much older than they were, besides being small and insignificant. Their comfortable world had been turned topsyturvy, and they needed to take it out on somebody...

The professor hadn't phoned; she realised that she had been counting on his coming at the weekend. It would be nice to be given an idea of how much longer she was to stay at Tisbury. Not that she wasn't content; the village was delightful, its few shops surprisingly up-market, the people friendly, but she was uneasy about Alice and her father. Since her mother's death she had automatically taken over the housekeeping, managed the finances of their day-to-day living and looked after Alice. Even when she had worked for the agency she had taken jobs which had allowed her to go home each evening.

An afternoon in the garden did much to restore her to her usual sensible self, and after supper Jimmy and Gloria went up to their rooms with their record-players and then to the sitting-room to watch television, and very much to her surprise made no demur when she went along presently and suggested that they went to bed.

She got up early the next morning; she supposed that they would go to church, and if they were to eat the shoulder of lamb for their lunch she would have to have it ready to put into the oven before they went. It was a bright morning and Tibs wandered off into the garden, following Mutt. She filled their saucers and left the door open for them to come back in and went to put on the kettle. A cup of tea would be a good start to her day...

She had laid the table ready for breakfast the night before; now she got out bacon, mushrooms and eggs and put the bread ready for the toaster.

Neither of the children was a quick dresser and she would have to look sharp if they were to get off to church. She made a pot of tea, donned an apron over her dressing-gown, rolled up her sleeves, and began to peel the potatoes.

She didn't turn round from the sink when she heard Mutt's claws on the ceramic tiles. 'Your breakfast is in your saucer,' she told him, 'and is Tibs with you?'

She put her knife down and took a drink from the cup of tea beside her and turned round. Professor Lister was leaning against the door-jamb, Tibs under one arm. He had had plenty of time to study her—hair hanging in a long shining curtain, the useful dressing-gown which did nothing for her tied round her small waist, the cuffs turned back...

He said, pleasantly impersonal, 'Good morning, Miss Smith. Forgive me for arriving at such an awkward hour. It was a last-minute decision to come...'

She wiped her hands and fetched another mug. 'Good morning, Professor Lister. The children are going to be delighted. Have a mug of tea—would you like something to eat? I can easily...'

'I'll share your breakfast, if I may, but tea would be delightful. Don't stop whatever you are doing. I'm sure that you have your hands full. Is everything all right?'

'Yes, thank you. If we are going to church, I need to get lunch ready to put in the oven before we go...'

He drank his tea and refilled their mugs. 'You have too much to do?' he wanted to know. 'Does Mrs Pretty not come?'

'Oh, yes—she's marvellous, and I'm not in the least overworked.' She tossed her hair over her shoulder and picked up another potato. 'You'll be here for lunch?'

'Certainly, and tea and supper if I may. I have had news from my sister—she phoned a few hours ago. The children will want to hear what she said.'

She put the potatoes into a saucepan and attacked a spring cabbage. 'Would you like me to call them now? They're not very quick at getting dressed.'

'Perhaps if I were to go up to their rooms and talk to them? That will give you a chance to get dressed...' His eyes swept over her person.

She suddenly went very red, and he wished he hadn't said that. He hadn't taken much notice of her, for the simple reason that there wasn't much to notice; now he hastened to make amends. 'I'll hurry them up a bit, shall I? If they are down before you are, they can make the toast and the tea.' He stood towering over her, smiling kindly, and a surge of rage swept through her.

What did he expect at seven o'clock in the morning? How dared he look at her like that, as though she were an object of pity? She said frostily, 'That seems a good idea, Professor.' She put the mugs tidily in the sink and went away without looking at him.

As she showered and dressed she could hear the children's excited voices from the other side of the landing and the rumble of their uncle's laughter. The news must be good, which meant that soon she would go home again. 'And a good thing too,' she told her reflection, as she pinned up her hair into a ruthless bun.

There was no one in the kitchen when she went downstairs; she put an apron on over her skirt and blouse and began to fry bacon.

They all came in together and Gloria said at once, 'You'll be able to go home soon, Araminta, our mother's coming home.'

'That's splendid news, and what a lovely surprise for you. Your father's better?'

She began to dish up eggs and mushrooms and bacon, and the professor came to take the plates from her. He switched on the toaster too, and told Gloria to pour the tea. 'My brother-in-law isn't well enough to come home yet, but he is making a good recovery and my sister feels able to return. He'll be flown back within the next week or so. Now it is just a question of Patty's return.'

'When Mother's back we shan't need Araminta,' said Jimmy.

The professor lifted his eyebrows. 'I think it very likely that your mother will be only too glad to have such a splendid helper. I do not dare to think how we would have managed without her help.'

Araminta, pecking at her bacon, didn't look up.

The talk was all of their mother's return and the prospect of seeing their father again, but breakfast was finished at last and the professor got up. 'Jimmy, take the plates over to the sink, will you? Gloria, put away the butter and the marmalade in the dresser. There are fifteen minutes before we need leave for church. Be ready in the hall, the pair of you, and see to Mutt and Tibs before we go, won't you?'

'Why didn't you bring Goldie and Neptune with you?' asked Gloria.

'I left home very early this morning. Buller will take them for a walk and I'll be home again this evening.'

He turned to Araminta. 'I'll wash the dishes if you want to get ready for church, Miss Smith.'

'Since you are here, do you mind if I stay at home? I'd be glad of an hour or two.'

'I upset you, didn't I? I'm sorry. You must be anxious to return to your own home, and I dare say the children have been difficult.'

She looked up at him. 'No, not at all. They have been very good, and I've been happy here.' She added tartly, 'I don't upset easily, Professor Lister.'

He said indifferently, 'Which, considering the work you do, must be a great advantage to you.'

With the place to herself she got the house tidied, made her own bed and, since neither Gloria nor Jimmy had done more than toss their duvets over the rumpled sheets, made theirs too, and then sped back to the kitchen to lay a tray for coffee before starting to prepare the lunch. She was usually a cheerful girl, but her thoughts were gloomy, and most of them centred on the professor. It was absurd that she should expect him to be more friendly; she was, after all, someone he had hired to do a job. He was invariably kind in an impersonal way, careful to treat her with courtesy, but all the same she was just Miss Smith to him, and that morning he had looked at her standing there in that old dressing-gown with her hair all over the place... She winced at what he must have thought. Anyway, she reminded herself, Mrs Gault would be home very soon now and that would be the end of it. The children would be glad to see her go—— She heard them coming into the house and put the milk on to boil.

'Uncle Jason's gone back to the Manor for drinks and coffee—he'll be here for lunch.' They threw their outdoor things down. 'Isn't coffee ready?'

'It will be by the time you've hung up your things.' It was no good being sharp with them, they had had too many years of spoiling, but at least they did as she asked, albeit grudgingly.

'We're going out after lunch—Uncle's going to take us to Bulbarrow for tea.'

Araminta poured the coffee and fetched the tin of biscuits. 'Isn't that a hill somewhere near Sturminster Newton?'

They looked surprised. 'Have you been there?'

'No, but there's an article about it in a magazine in the sitting-room. You'll be able to take Mutt.'

They went off to their rooms presently and she got on with her cooking; presumably the professor would want his lunch when he got back. She laid the table, wondering if she should use the dining-room. She and the children had had all their meals in the kitchen and there didn't seem much point in using another room. She was hesitating about getting out the good china when he came wandering in.

'We've been eating in the kitchen—not just breakfast, but all the time. I expect you'd rather have lunch in the dining-room?'

'No, no. I find the kitchen very pleasant. Is lunch ready? We're going to Bulbarrow this afternoon, no great distance, but the children are bound to want their tea there. There's a nice little place—Dorset cream teas and so on.'

'I'll dish up while you have a drink, Professor.'

'We'll both have a drink. Lady Scobell at the Manor is charming, but I swear she gave us all cooking sherry.'

He went away and returned a few minutes later with two glasses of sherry. 'Something smells delicious,' he observed, and added, 'You'll come with us, of course.'

'I think not, Professor. The children are fond of you and want you to themselves.'

'Oh, I'm not sure about that.' He glanced at her. 'But if you prefer to stay here, please do. Have a quiet few hours free with a book.'

She assured him happily that she would do just that; she would also get the supper ready, do the last of the ironing and write home. She longed to go with him, but her enjoyment would be spoilt since the children would resent her being with them. It would spoil the afternoon for everyone.

Sherry had sent a little spurt of pleasure through her, so that she reminded herself not to wallow in self-pity. On a wave of sherry-induced cheerfulness she dished up and called the children to the table.

She was a good cook: the shoulder of lamb was just right, the roast potatoes were crisp on the outside and meltingly floury inside, and there were baby carrots and creamed spinach. She watched the professor carve and said apologetically, 'I'm sorry it's lamb again, but I didn't know that you were coming and Jimmy and Gloria like it best.'

'And so do I. You will make some lucky man a good wife, Miss Smith.'

He didn't see the children look down at their plates to hide their smiles, but Araminta did. She said airily, 'Yes, I shall enjoy being married and having a home of my own.'

She had the satisfaction of seeing their surprise. The professor looked surprised too, and rather thoughtful.

The professor insisted that everyone should help clear away the dishes and help with the washing-up before they left the house, and only when the last plate had been put away did he go out to the car.

'We should be back some time after five o'clock,' he told Araminta. 'Could we have supper around half-past seven? I'd like to leave at nine o'clock.'

He nodded a cheerful goodbye and she watched the car skim down the drive and into the lane, then she went back into the house and, since she had no wish to sit and think, got out her pastry board and made a batch of sausage rolls. She made a custard tart too, for afters. None of that took very long and the afternoon stretched emptily before her. The ironing could wait, she decided; she would find a book and get a jacket and sit in the garden for a while. It was a pleasant afternoon, still cool, but the sun shone and there were sheltered nooks where she could sit.

Tibs joined her, sitting beside her on the bench, and presently she closed her eyes and her book and allowed her thoughts to roam, and since there was no one to whom she could talk she talked to Tibs.

'This job has unsettled me,' she reflected. 'I dare say it's partly the children—naturally they don't like me, I'm all part and parcel of the upheaval, aren't I? And, to be honest, I do not like these jobs. I would like to do something worthwhile and be very good at it so that people said, "There's that clever Miss Smith," and I'd have enough money to buy lovely clothes...' She thought for a bit. 'And a different face!'

Tibs gave her a thoughtful glance and returned to her toilette; as far as she was concerned, her manner implied, Araminta could be cross-eyed and ten feet tall; she was the one who remembered to fill her saucer at the right times.

They both went indoors presently, to their respective teas, and shortly afterwards the others came back. Araminta, waging her usual obstinate battle over the hanging of garments on the hooks provided, hoped politely that they had enjoyed their afternoon, and was surprised to be answered just as politely, unaware that their uncle had expressed his displeasure at their casual treatment of her, and when they followed her into the kitchen and offered to help, she decided that the day hadn't been so bad after all.

He came into the house then, and they had their supper, and when the meal was over, obedient to their uncle's wish, they went upstairs to their rooms to play their loud music and watch the television.

As the first raucous notes floated down the stairs, Professor Lister asked, 'How can you bear it?'

'Well, actually, I can't, but it is their house, isn't it? And it's only for an hour or so in the evenings.'

'You enjoyed your few hours of peace?' He had sat down at the table. 'Please come and sit down, there are one or two matters...'

She sat. 'I've kept an account of the money I've spent,' she began.

'Yes, yes, don't bother with that. You'll need some more money—remind me before I go.' He stared at her across the table and she looked back at him enquiringly.

'Do you dislike me, Miss Smith?'

'Good heavens, no,' said Araminta. 'In fact I quite like you. Not that I know you, if you see what I mean. But that doesn't really matter, does it? I mean, we aren't likely to meet again once Mrs Gault comes home.'

He didn't answer that. 'You said that you were looking forward to getting married. Was that true?'

She looked at him in surprise, going rather red. 'No.'

'I am relieved to hear it. Have you no ambitions? Do you not wish to be a career girl?'

'Me?' She smiled. 'I don't look like one, do I? They are tall and thin, and wear those severe suits with very short skirts.'

He observed blandly, 'You have very nice legs, Miss Smith.' His eyes were on her face. Why, she wondered, had she ever thought that he was absent-minded? He was staring at her like a hawk. 'So your future is an open book...'

'Well, yes, until the next job turns up.' On an impulse she asked, 'Why do you call me Miss Smith? No one else ever does.'

He smiled then. 'It suits you!' He glanced at his watch. 'I should be going.' He fished in his pocket, took out his notecase and handed her some notes. 'That should keep you going for a few more days. Let me know how things are when I phone. I had better say goodbye to the children.'

The three of them watched him drive away, and Araminta, remembering their conversation, tried to make head or tail of it and couldn't.

CHAPTER FOUR

LATER, in bed that night, Araminta thought about the professor. He had asked her some strange questions. Whatever difference did it make to him whether she liked him or not? And why should he be relieved to hear that she wasn't going to get married? Had he another job in mind for her and, if so, why hadn't he said so? He was really rather nice; indeed, if she allowed herself to do so, she could easily wish to see more of him, which was absurd, for they had very little to say to each other during their infrequent meetings. She knew nothing about him. For all she knew, he might be engaged...

He wasn't a young man...

She went to sleep at last and dreamed about him.

The professor didn't dream of her, but he found himself thinking about her as he drove back to his home. He knew considerably more about her than she did about him, and for some reason he found it difficult to dismiss her image from his mind. Perhaps because she was so unlike any of the women of his acquaintance. She had made no attempt to engage his attention; the reverse, in fact. He had found himself disappointed when she had refused to go with him and the children to Bulbarrow. She was refreshingly undemanding and he no longer found her plain. How pleasant, he considered, to be able to read and study in his library without the fear of phone calls begging him to dine or escort any of his women acquaintances, wasting hours of precious leisure listening to female chatter; a happy state which could be achieved if he were to marry a girl as undemanding as Araminta. He laughed aloud then, and dismissed the absurd idea.

There was little traffic; he was home soon after eleven o'clock, to be greeted by Buller with sandwiches and coffee and the dogs. He went straight into the garden with them, and then went to his study to sit back in his chair with a glass of whisky in his hand and the dogs at his feet—an hour of peaceful reading a pleasant prospect.

He had barely turned a page when the phone rang and he put his book down resignedly. At that hour it would be the hospital...

It wasn't the hospital. 'Jason,' screamed a voice, 'I've been phoning the whole evening. I'm at the Redvers'— it's her birthday, and you simply must come along. I suppose you've got your head in a book? Darling, you simply must come. It's ages since I've seen you.'

The professor frowned. 'I'm just home after a very long day, Vicky. And I've a very busy day tomorrow.'

'Oh, Jason, you are a staid old stick. You might just as well be married for all the fun you are!'

'Sorry, Vicky. There must be any number of young men falling over themselves to get at you.'

'Well, yes, there are. I'll leave you to your bed and book—there is a book there, I'll swear?'

He laughed. 'Yes. I dare say I'll see you some time.'

'Good. Marjorie had lunch with me the other day. She would love us to get married, you know.'

'Yes. I do know.'

It was a moment or two before she said, 'Oh, well, goodnight, Jason.'

'Goodnight, Vicky.' He put down the receiver with relief. Vicky was a dear girl, he had known her for years, since she had gone to the same school as his sister Marjorie and spent several holidays at his home, and later he had met her again from time to time. It had never entered his head to marry her; she was pretty and empty-headed and worked part-time in a boutique, and from time to time she phoned him, demanding to be taken to the theatre or out to dinner.

He picked up his book again, reflecting that if he were married... That nonsensical idea he had had driving up from Tisbury wasn't as silly as it seemed.

He didn't get back from the hospital until the early evening on the next day, intent on taking the dogs for a run in the park, but first he would have to phone Araminta. No need for a long talk, he told himself, just a routine enquiry as to the day, which was why he sounded impatient to Araminta when she picked up the phone.

It had been a typical Monday for her: several loads of washing, the ironing, shopping, Mutt to take for a walk, a meal to cook and the children, now that their mother was coming home, more boisterous than usual. Her 'hello' was decidedly snappy.

'Everything is all right?' he wanted to know.

She looked at the basket overflowing with school shirts and blouses, sports kit, sheets and pillowcases, endless towels... She said frostily. 'Yes, thank you.'

'Children behaving?'

'Yes, thank you. They are doing their homework.'

'Good. Goodbye, Miss Smith.'

He spent an hour in the park, dismissing from his mind the idea that Miss Smith had been decidedly cross. He went home presently and had his dinner, and then spent the evening by the fire, the dogs at his feet, reading the newspaper and dipping into Homer's *Iliad*, and presently going to his study to make notes for a lecture he was to give at the next seminar.

He spent the whole of the following morning in his consulting-rooms in Harley Street before going to the hospital for a ward round. He got home earlier than usual, to find Buller waiting for him in the hall.

'Mrs Gault telephoned, sir, not an hour ago. She's leaving in the morning and should be at Heathrow the day after tomorrow. She will ring again this evening.'

'Splendid, Buller. She isn't likely to ring for an hour or so, I should imagine. I'll take the dogs out straight away. If she should ring, ask her what time her plane gets in and say I'll meet it or arrange for her to be met.'

It was much later in the evening when Mrs Gault phoned again, which gave the professor time to adjust his appointments for Thursday as far as possible. Her flight would get in at six o'clock in the evening and, despite her eagerness to go home, she consented to spend the night at his house and be driven down early in the morning.

'But I shan't see the children—they'll be at school...'

'Suppose we drive down really early? In time for breakfast? You can see them before they leave, spend the day unpacking and getting settled in, and be there when they get home at teatime.'

'Can you spare the time to take me home, Jason?'

'Yes, provided we leave here about half-past five. I must be back by one o'clock; I've several private patients to see.'

'You're an angel. Everything's all right, isn't it?' She sounded anxious.

'Perfectly, my dear.' He put down the phone and sat for a moment thinking. He could, of course, ring Araminta, but it was late evening by now; she might be in bed and asleep. If she wasn't, she might find it necessary to go around dusting and cleaning, anxious to have everything spick and span. He would have to explain about Patty and see what his sister wanted to do, and then he could leave everything to her. He went back to his medical journal with a sigh of relief.

Mrs Gault's plane was on time; he watched her hurrying through the crowds. She hadn't bothered with a trolley but lugged a case in each hand, and he went to meet her and take them from her.

'Jason.' She was bubbling over with excitement. 'Oh, it's marvellous to be home again—you've no idea—no proper loos and such strange food... Tom's fine, he's flying back next week.' She flung her arms round him and gave him a sisterly kiss. 'You're a darling to meet me. Has it been awful? The children, I mean, and no Patty. How have you managed?'

He had stowed her bags and urged her into the car before getting in beside her. 'I haven't—I found a treasure in Miss Smith, who's been looking after the children and running the house.'

'Oh, how clever of you. What's she like? I was too upset to notice.'

'Plain,' said the professor. 'Nicely plump, large dark eyes and a very direct manner.'

Mrs Gault stole a look at his profile and saw that he was smiling. She said mildly, 'She sounds just right. Do the children like her?'

'Not particularly. They resent her, you see—naturally enough—no Patty to let them do exactly as they like, so they treat her like a servant. Which doesn't appear to bother her in the least.'

'They can be tiresome,' said their fond mother. 'Teen-agers, you know.' She added, 'Well, I'm grateful to your treasure, but it will be nice when Patty can come back.'

'You can phone her this evening and see how she is. I'm sure Miss Smith will stay until Patty returns.' He stopped the car in front of his house. 'Mrs Buller has laid on a splendid dinner for us this evening—you're not too tired to enjoy it?'

'I'm tired, but I'm longing for something to eat. I was too excited on the plane.'

Presently, after the splendid dinner, they sat on either side of the fire in the drawing-room, Goldie and Neptune between them.

'Have you done anything interesting while I've been away?' asked Mrs Gault.

The professor said mildly, 'My dear Lydia, if by that you mean have I been out and about, wining and dining lady-friends and seeing the latest plays, then no, I have done nothing interesting. Vicky phoned and wanted me to go to some party or other, but I was only just back from Tisbury—oh, and Marjorie phoned, wanted to know when you would be back.'

Lydia said quickly, 'What an idiot I am. Of course, you've been going down to Tisbury as well as all the other things you do. You've not had a minute to yourself, have you? How's the hospital?'

'Bursting at the seams. I enjoyed keeping an eye on the children, my dear.' He glanced at his watch. 'If we're to leave early, I think you should go to bed.'

She yawned. 'I can't wait. What about you, Jason?'

'I'm going to the hospital. I shan't be long.' He walked with her to the stairs. 'Sleep well. It's splendid to have you home again and to know that Tom is well.'

She leaned up to kiss his cheek. 'I'm so grateful, Jason, and once I'm home I promise I'll leave you in peace. You can go back to your books and the dogs and your never-ending work. Are you never lonely?'

He smiled. 'I'm too busy.'

Which wasn't quite true, he reflected as he got into his car. He hadn't realised until just lately that he needed someone to talk to, someone who would listen. Someone, he had to admit, who would leave him in peace to read or to write during his hard-won leisure and not pester him to attend the various social functions he did his best to avoid.

'What you need,' his sister had said with sudden vigour, 'is a wife. You're fast becoming a crusty old bachelor.'

They left before it was light the next morning. It was a typical March day, with a fierce chilly wind and clouds scudding across a dark sky, but it was quite warm in the car and the dogs curled up and slept almost at once, leaving Lydia to talk excitedly as the professor drove through the almost empty streets and away from the city. Once away from it he drove steadily at the maximum speed; there was little traffic going west, and it was barely seven o'clock when he turned off the A303 and took the minor road to Tisbury.

There were lights shining from the village as he swept through its main street and presently turned off into the lane and in at his sister's gate. There were lights shining from the windows here too.

'I'd love a cup of tea,' said Mrs Gault in a shaky voice. 'I don't suppose they're up yet.'

'Perhaps not the children, but I imagine Miss Smith is going about her duties.'

As they got out of the car Lydia said, 'I hope she won't think that we're spying on her.'

He had turned away to let the dogs out. 'Most unlikely.'

'She has got another name, you know. You call her Miss Smith all the time?'

The professor took her arm. 'I think we had better knock...'

Araminta, trotting from room to room pulling back curtains and opening windows, went to open the door. The postman, she supposed, with something too large to go through the letter-box.

She flung the door wide. 'Mrs Gault—what a lovely surprise.' She smiled with delight. 'Won't the children...? You'd like a cup of tea while I get them up.' She re-arranged her unassuming features into a polite and rather small smile. 'Good morning, Professor Lister. The kitchen's warm. I'll make the tea.'

The professor said deliberately, 'Good morning, Miss Smith. Tea would be delightful.' He took his sister's coat and tossed it on to a chair. It was barely half-past seven in the morning and Araminta looked as fresh as the proverbial daisy. No make-up, he noted, and her hair had been tied back with an elastic ribbon and, as far as he remembered, she was wearing the same sensible and dull clothes, and yet he had to admit she was pleasing to the eye.

Mrs Gault was sitting by the Aga weeping quietly. 'Don't mind me,' she told her brother, 'I'm so happy.'

'Of course you are,' he told her kindly. 'Shall you wait here until the children come down to breakfast?'

Mrs Gault looked at Araminta, who said in her matter-of-fact way, 'I'll call them about now—usually they have to be ready to leave by eight o'clock, but there's some kind of meeting for both schools today and they don't have to be there before half-past nine. Mrs Sloane takes them.'

The professor said easily, 'I'll drop them off as I go. Remind me to ring Mrs Sloane.'

Araminta said, 'Yes, Professor Lister,' and nipped upstairs to call the children; their mother could hear their indignant voices at being roused, followed by reassuring bumps and thumps as they got themselves out of their beds.

Araminta, already back in the kitchen, got out the frying-pan, bacon, eggs and mushrooms, and busied herself at the Aga, and when she would have collected plates and cutlery for Mrs Gault and the professor he got to his feet. 'I'll do that—do you want bread cut for toast?'

'Yes, please.' Araminta inspected her rashers and gave the mushrooms a prod, and Mrs Gault looked with astonishment at her brother, who, to the best of her knowledge, was the least domesticated of men.

'Perhaps you would fill the kettle,' said Araminta. 'The children will be down in a few minutes now.'

'A sensible girl, reflected Lydia, no nonsense about her, and she was making no effort to attract Jason's attention, although she was perfectly polite towards him. As for him—despite the coolness of his manner towards her, he was by no means indifferent... Interesting, thought Lydia, and turned a smiling face to the door as her children bounded in.

The meal was naturally enough a boisterous one, both children talking together and asking questions, wanting to know everything at once. If the professor noticed that they ignored Araminta almost entirely, he said nothing, and when Gloria said suddenly, 'I've torn my leotard,

Araminta, and I have to have it for school,' and added, 'It's on my bed,' he watched Araminta slip away with a murmured excuse, unnoticed by the other three.

Presently Gloria, aware of his eyes upon her, looked across the table at him. He raised an eyebrow. 'Aren't you old enough to do your own sewing?' he mildly wanted to know, and she had the grace to blush.

'Araminta's here to look after us,' she muttered, 'she's paid...'

'Anyone who works gets paid,' observed her uncle blandly. 'I get paid too.'

Araminta came back presently, while they were sitting and talking at the table. 'Your leotard's on the bed,' she said, and began to clear the table. 'And will you both go and make your beds quickly? Your mother is tired and I've no doubt that she will want to rest today.'

'But you're here,' said Jimmy. 'You can do the beds...'

'Well, no. You see, now your mother is home there is no need for me to stay. I must get packed—I'd like to get an afternoon train.'

The children gaped at her. 'But you can't; Patty's not here.'

'I'm sure she'll be back very soon, and Mrs Pretty comes today.' Araminta looked at Mrs Gault. 'Everything's as you would like it, I hope. I'll do any shopping this morning, while Mrs Pretty is here. The arrangement was that I should stay until you returned.'

'Of course,' Mrs Gault agreed. 'I'm sure everything is in apple-pie order. I'll phone Patty and see when we can expect her back.' She smiled at Araminta. 'I am so grateful to you, especially as you've had to stay much longer than you had expected. Of course you can go this afternoon—you must be anxious to get home.'

The professor hadn't said a word, sitting in his chair listening. Now he spoke. 'Would you consider staying overnight, Miss Smith? That would be a great help to my sister. I'll come for you tomorrow morning—around nine o'clock, if that suits you?'

'That is very kind of you,' said Araminta 'but it's a long way to come just to fetch me, and there are plenty of trains.'

'Ah, but I need to see somebody at Odstock Hospital—the appointment is for eight o'clock, which gives me ample time to drive on here by nine.' He glanced at her. 'Not too early for you?'

'Me? No—no, of course not. Thank you very much, Professor Lister.'

'Oh, good,' said Mrs Gault. 'I must confess it will be nice to have you here until tomorrow.' She smiled at her brother. 'Thank you for bringing me home, Jason, and for taking such good care of everything while I was away—it was like a nightmare, you know.'

'Over now, my dear.' He stood up. 'If Jimmy and Gloria are ready, we'll be on our way. I'll see you both tomorrow.'

He collected the dogs, called to the children, kissed his sister's cheek, gave Araminta a brief nod and drove away.

Mrs Gault went upstairs to unpack while Araminta washed up and tidied the kitchen. Jason had been very carefully off-hand with Araminta and yet there was something...

'"Miss Smith", indeed!' She snorted. 'She's really rather sweet.'

Mrs Pretty came presently, delighted to be the first in the village to know that Mrs Gault was back, and lavish in her praise of Araminta's housekeeping. 'Proper little housewife she is, and looked after the kids too.'

She drank the strong tea and started on the kitchen, and Mrs Gault and Araminta took a tray of coffee into the sitting-room. 'I've kept accounts of what I've spent,' said Araminta, 'and the rest of the money Professor Lister gave me is in the dresser drawer.'

Mrs Gault wasn't interested in the household expenses. 'Tell me, my dear, were the children good at their uncle's? Poor man, he's used to a quiet life when he's not working. I'd better phone Patty.'

She came back into the room looking frankly relieved. 'Patty's mother died two days ago. I'm so sorry for Patty, but her mother was old and had Alzheimer's disease, so it was a happy release. Patty is coming back directly after the funeral—in three days' time.' She added apologetically, 'She's been with us for years—I'm lost without her.'

Araminta said, 'The children love her, don't they? It's nice that she has you to come back to and to know that she's wanted.'

'I'm eternally grateful to you, Araminta. I hope being here hasn't disrupted your life in any way?'

'No, not at all. Though I usually take jobs where I can go home each day...'

'You have parents, or do you live on your own?'

'I have a father and a younger sister.'

'My dear, you must ring them and tell them you'll be home tomorrow. I'm not sure when, though.' She frowned. 'Jason didn't say, did he?'

'Well, it doesn't matter. I'll be home round about noon, I expect—plenty of time to do the shopping and cook the supper.' She stood up. 'I'll just pop down to the butcher. What would you like for supper, Mrs Gault?

And wouldn't you like to have a nap for an hour? I'll call you in good time for lunch. Mrs Pretty goes around one o'clock—would it do if I had lunch ready for just after that?'

'Something light. Don't go to a lot of trouble, my dear. You'll need some time to pack. There won't be much time in the morning; Jason is always so punctual.'

So Araminta took herself off to the village shops, buying with a prudent eye and saying her goodbyes with some reluctance; she had grown attached to the charming place during the two weeks she had been there. She had a mug of tea with Mrs Pretty when she got back, fending off that lady's searching questions as to her future with gentle vagueness.

There were several jobs to keep her busy for the rest of that day, and, supper over and cleared away, she excused herself with the plea that she still had to finish her packing and went to her room; the children hadn't had much of a chance to talk to their mother, nor she to them.

She washed her hair and then lay in a too-hot bath, thinking about the future. There would be quite a nice sum of money to collect from the agency, but most of it would have to go into the household purse. She only hoped that Alice hadn't been running up bills... She would have to take the next job she was offered, but it would have to be one where she could go to and fro each day. She felt no enthusiasm for that, and turned her thoughts to the drive back to London with Professor Lister. A strange man—reserved, wrapped up much too tightly in his work, and yet kind. She liked him, despite the fact that he didn't appear to like her—no, she had that wrong, he had never displayed any feelings towards her save gratitude, and that in an absent-minded fashion.

He arrived at nine o'clock, bade her good morning, made his unhurried farewells, assured his sister that he would be down to see her as soon as he could spare the time, popped Araminta into the car, got in and drove away. They had been driving for some time and were on the A303 before he spoke.

'Whereabouts is your agency?' And when she told him, he said, 'We'll call there on our way, shall we, and you can collect whatever is owing to you?'

'How kind, but there is no need. I can go this afternoon or tomorrow morning.'

His grunt left her uncertain as to whether he agreed with her. 'You will take a few days off?'

'Well, not if there's a job available where I can go home each day.'

'Perhaps if your sister has been sufficiently reassured by her doctor, she will find something to do.' His voice was dry.

'Well, I don't know what,' said Araminta forthrightly. 'She isn't trained for anything, you see.'

'Neither are you, Miss Smith.'

A remark which she felt put her neatly in her place. She had no intention of replying to it but sat composedly, watching the scenery flash past.

As they neared Fleet service station, he asked, 'Coffee? Breakfast seems a long while ago,' and turned the car into the vast car-park.

The place was crowded but he found a small table for two, sat her down at it and went to fetch the coffee. They drank it in friendly silence and without waste of time, and as they got up to go he said easily, 'I'll be in the car—come when you're ready.'

Thankfully Araminta sped to the ladies'.

As they approached the outskirts of the city, she asked, 'Would it be more convenient for you to put me down at a bus-stop? I dare say you're busy and I have all day.'

'So have I until late this afternoon. I'll take you home, Araminta.'

The Rolls drew up soundlessly before her house and the professor got out, opened her door, and crossed the narrow pavement beside her, waiting while she got out her key and unlocked the door. The little house felt chilly and rather damp. It was quiet too.

'Alice,' called Araminta. 'Alice?' And she poked her head round the sitting-room door. The room was empty and extremely untidy and dusty. She withdrew her head and turned to the professor. 'There's no one at home. Would you like some coffee?' She hoped she didn't sound as unwilling as she felt to let him see the sitting-room— and the kitchen would be worse.

Professor Lister had taken in the air of neglect, the faint smell of a meal which hung in it, the film of dust on the small table in the hall. He was filled with a pitying concern—to come home to such a place—no welcome, and that didn't mean that there had to be someone there, but a cheerful and clean house, a few flowers, a nice feeling that someone would be back home soon. Araminta was making the best of it, although he suspected that once she was alone she would burst into tears...

He hadn't gone into the agency with her; she had come out looking cheerful, with the observation that there was a job waiting for her only a short bus-ride from her home. He had asked her to have lunch with him then, but she had declined quietly and he hadn't pressed her. He wished now that he had. He said, carefully casual,

'Well, since there is no one at home, I suggest you come with me and we'll find somewhere to eat.'

'You're very kind,' she told him, 'but if you don't mind I'd better stay here. I expect Alice is shopping; she might be home at any minute.' She smiled rather shyly. 'It was very kind of you to bring me home. I'm most grateful.'

He studied her quiet face for a moment. 'I'll get your bag,' he said.

Which he did, setting it down in the narrow hall, towering over her. 'I—my sister and I—are most grateful to you, Miss Smith. I hope that you will be able to take a few days off before you take another job.'

'Oh, I shall,' she told him earnestly, not meaning a word of it. She put out a hand and had it engulfed in his large, firm grip. 'I enjoyed it, you know—Tisbury was lovely; to open the door in the morning and see nothing but green fields outside.' Her eyes were on the row of identical red-brick houses opposite. She said too brightly, 'Goodbye, Professor Lister.'

To his astonishment he found himself wishing to kiss her, but he didn't, merely released her hand, smiled and got back into his car. He drove away without looking back.

'That's that,' said Araminta, and shut the door behind her, took her bag upstairs and went down to the kitchen. It was a miserable little place in any case, now made much worse by the dirty dishes waiting to be washed, used pans on the grimy stove and a floor sadly in need of a good scrub, let alone a sweep. She was hungry, but she couldn't eat until she had cleared up the mess. She got her pinny from behind the kitchen door and set to work. There wasn't time to do all that needed to be done, but the dishes were washed, the stove wiped clean and the floor swept and mopped. She made herself some tea then, found bread and butter and cheese and sat down to eat it before going along to the sitting-room. She had restored it to a dusted and tidy state when Alice came back. She stood in the doorway, looking at Araminta. 'So you're back, and high time too. Living off the fat of the land, I suppose, while I slave away in this beastly place.'

'Hello, Alice. I didn't let you know I would be back because I wasn't sure what time we'd get here.'

'We? Who's we?'

'Professor Lister gave me a lift.'

Alice flung her coat and a plastic shopping-bag on to a chair. 'And I missed him. Is he coming again?'

'No, why should he? The job's finished. The agency has another one for me—mornings. Nine o'clock until noon. It's ten minutes from the bus.'

'Well, I hope you've got some money. There's the butcher and greengrocer to pay—I've been running up bills.'

'Surely Father gave you the housekeeping...'

'I spent most of it on a jacket—it looks just like leather, and I just had to have it.'

'Supposing I tell you that I haven't been paid,' said Araminta.

Alice shrugged. 'We'll just have to keep on running up bills. I'm glad you're back because you can do that.'

She's my sister and I must love her, thought Araminta desperately. 'Did you go to the doctor?'

'Yes, but only because that heavenly man told me to.'

'And what did he say?'

Alice said sulkily, 'He said that I should have gone months ago to see him.'

'So there's nothing wrong with you?'

'That's what he said, but I'm delicate—Father says so.'

'All the same, you'll have to find a job, Alice, with enough money so that you don't use the housekeeping. And this place was like a pigsty.'

Alice eyed her with astonishment. 'Good Lord, what's come over you? I shan't do anything of the sort; there's enough with you and Father working. I'll look after the house.'

'But you don't, do you, Alice?'

'Well, it's so boring, isn't it? What's for lunch?'

'I had a sandwich. What have you got for supper tonight?'

'Steak—Father fancied that—it's on the bill, so I didn't have to pay for it.'

Araminta bit back the words on her tongue. What would be the use of getting angry? 'I'm going to unpack and do a load of washing and then the ironing.' She started for the door.

'There are a lot of Father's shirts,' began Alice.

'I shan't be long. You can put in a load after mine and do the ironing tomorrow morning while I'm at work.'

Alice stared at her. 'What's come over you, Araminta? You like housework; you've been doing it for years.'

'Yes, and I expect I shall go on doing it for years to come, but I get paid from the agency—I've never been paid here, have I?' Araminta spoke in a matter-of-fact voice. 'Now I really must get ready for the morning—you'll see to supper?'

But, when she went downstairs with a load of washing for the machine, Alice had gone, leaving a note on the kitchen table. She had promised a friend that she would go to the cinema and she wouldn't be home until the evening.

So Araminta cooked the supper and greeted her father when he got home.

'You're back.' He kissed her cheek. 'I'm glad to see you, my dear. Alice really isn't up to running a house, you know. Did you get paid?'

Araminta was laying the table. 'Yes, Father. I'll go tomorrow afternoon and pay the bills, if you'll let me have them, and I shall need some housekeeping money.'

'Things are a bit tight—there have been one or two expenses ... You've enough to tide us over?'

'I don't think so. I'll settle as many bills as I can. Father, now that Alice is as fit as you or I, she should get a job too and help out. Don't you agree?'

'Well, my dear, Alice isn't cut out for hard work. Surely between us we can manage to keep her at home? She's such a pretty girl she's sure to get a good husband, especially now she's going out and about quite a bit.'

Araminta dished up. She wanted to scream, throw something, break a few bits of china; she was back on the treadmill again with no hope of escaping. She could earn just enough from the agency to keep them solvent, and even when Alice married, as she was certain to do, she herself would have to stay at home to look after the house and her father. She said in a quiet little voice, 'Supper's ready, Father. Alice has gone out with friends.'

'She deserves a little jaunt. I must say, Araminta, that leaving us to fend for ourselves was rather unkind of you.'

There was no answer to that. Presently, after supper, she did the ironing while her father watched television, and then she went to bed, where she cried herself to sleep because she was unhappy. 'The unfairness of life,' she mumbled into her pillow. 'Being plain and poor and condemned to endless household chores and never going to see Professor Lister again.'

She was up early to cook the breakfast and then leave to catch her bus. Alice wasn't down yet and her father had hardly spoken to her, and that, she knew, was because she hadn't given him any of her earnings. She had added up the bills she had found stuffed in a drawer and the total shocked her; there was no question of giving him any money, although being a still-loving daughter she felt guilty about it, but if she had given way to his wishes no bills would have been paid, she was sure of that.

The address she had been given was in a quiet street in Bloomsbury, one of a terrace of tall Victorian houses with basements with barred widows. It looked well-cared-for, and that cheered her. The agency had told her that she was needed to assist the house-owner with her elderly mother, and the pay was quite good. She mounted the steps and rang the bell.

CHAPTER FIVE

THE door was opened by a woman with a grubby apron and an even grubbier pair of hands. 'You're the new help?' She nodded her head over her shoulder. 'Come on in and good luck to you, ducks.'

She stood aside and Araminta went past her into a wide hall, handsomely papered and thickly carpeted. 'She's in 'ere,' said the woman, and opened a door.

It was a large room, made small by the amount of old-fashioned heavy furniture in it. The curtains were half drawn so that it was gloomy and, as the window was shut, Araminta was met by a wave of cold stuffy air.

The woman gave her a poke in the back. 'Mrs Taylor will be along, ducks,' and closed the door behind her.

Araminta walked into the centre of the room and peered around. There was a narrow bed pushed into the corner of the room, and she went towards it. Presumably the hump in it was a person. Araminta said 'Good morning,' and wondered if she should pull the curtains. The door opened and a youngish woman came in, crossed to the window, pulled back the curtains and turned to look at Araminta.

'I hope you're strong,' she said, and then added, 'You are from the agency?'

'Yes, good morning.' Araminta supposed that she should have added 'madam' but she wasn't going to; the woman was ill-mannered and Araminta, with enough to worry about, wasn't inclined to be meek.

The woman nodded towards the bed. 'My mother—
she has to be got up, washed and dressed, and sat in her
chair. You'll clean the room and make up the bed, light
the fire and see that she has a hot drink. Mrs Loder goes
at half-past eleven. If I'm not back, you'll have to wait
until I get home.'

'The agency told me that the hours were nine o'clock
until noon.'

'That's right. I hope you're not a clock-watcher.
There's a cloakroom off the hall; you can wash Mrs Price
there. You'll find all you need in the kitchen at the end
of the hall. I'll see you when I get back.'

Not very satisfactory, reflected Araminta, and took a
good look at the room before going to introduce herself
to the occupant of the bed.

The furniture was good, even if too large, but it was
dusty and dull from lack of polishing. There was ash in
the fireplace behind the high fire-guard, and a pile of
newspapers on one of the chairs. She advanced to the
bed. Her 'Good morning, Mrs Price,' was greeted with
a grunt, and an elderly, ill-tempered face peered at her
from a tumbled bed.

'I've come to help you,' said Araminta. 'I will help
you wash and dress and tidy up a bit.' She eyed the bedlinen. 'And put clean sheets on the bed.'

'I don't want to get up. I'm very comfortable as I am.'

'Well, if I'm going to make the bed I'm afraid you'll
have to get out of it, and you'll feel much more the thing
once you are in a chair.'

Araminta, wheedling the old lady to get from her bed,
wondered why the agency hadn't told her that it was
really a job for someone with nursing experience. It took
the best part of an hour to get Mrs Price to walk to the
cloakroom, get her washed and dressed, and then sitting

in a chair while Araminta brushed her sparse white hair. 'I'm cold,' said Mrs Price.

Araminta rummaged in a drawer and found a shawl. 'I'll get the fire lighted,' she promised.

That took some time; Mrs Loder had to be found and asked where brushes and bucket, firewood and coals were kept, and the ashes had to be swept up and carted away. 'And I want clean sheets,' said Araminta firmly as she came back into the house from the back yard, 'and the vacuum cleaner and dusters.'

'New brooms sweep clean,' said Mrs Loder, 'and mind you remember that I'm off when me time's up and not a minute longer.'

Araminta lighted the fire, made a warm drink for Mrs Price, and began on the bed. She wondered when the sheets had last been changed, and got great satisfaction from the sight of the nicely made bed when she had finished it. She dumped the used linen in the cloakroom and set about vacuuming, and by then it was almost twelve o'clock. She flew round with a duster, tut-tutting at the dirt and at the same time engaging the old lady in conversation. 'Do you go out at all?'

'Me? No, Miss Nosy, I don't. I prefer to stay here in my own room, although my daughter can't find a sensible woman to clean the place and attend to my wants, and I don't know why.'

'We're hard to find,' said Araminta mildly, and longed for five minutes peace and a cup of coffee.

Twelve o'clock came and went and there was no sign of Mrs Taylor. It was half an hour later by the time she returned. She came into the room, nodded to her mother and observed, 'You found everything then.' Her eyes lighted on the bed. 'Clean sheets—surely not necessary...?'

'The bedlinen was filthy,' said Araminta, and had the satisfaction of seeing Mrs Taylor's face grow red.

'You put everything in the washing-machine, I hope? There'll be time for you to iron it tomorrow.'

'It's in the cloakroom, and I'll do the ironing if you wish me to, Mrs Taylor, but then I won't have time to do anything for Mrs Price.'

Mrs Taylor's ample bosom swelled visibly. 'Three hours is ample time to do the little there is to do for my mother. Since you are new to the job, I'll ask Mrs Loder to do the ironing. Be here punctually in the morning, Miss Smith.'

She went out of the room, which was as well, for Araminta was on the point of giving her employer the same advice.

There was no sign of Alice when she got home, although there were the remains of a snack lunch on the table. Araminta, feeling grubby after her morning's chores, washed and changed before sitting down to her own lunch. She didn't linger over it, but collected the bills, fetched her purse and shopping-bag, and walked to the row of small shops at the end of the street. She wouldn't be able to pay them all; she would need to keep some of the money back until such time as her father let her have more. She went in and out of the various shops, paying everyone something and buying food suitable to the household budget. Now that she was home each day there would be no need to buy the fast foods Alice had found so convenient.

Alice was still not home when she got back. She prepared a casserole, made a bread-and-butter pudding, and took her tea into the sitting-room, and while she drank it she wondered about Professor Lister. Would she ever see him again? she wondered. She began to dream, letting her tea get cold—appendicitis and rushed dramatically to hospital for immediate operation, and when she came round from the anaesthetic, there he would be, bending over her, reassuring her that she would recover, that she was a marvellous patient, that her courage in the face of pain had quite won his heart...

'Well, really,' declared Araminta loudly, 'I need my head examined—of all the nonsense.' She added with determined briskness, 'He'll have forgotten me completely by now.'

But he hadn't.

Her father came home presently. 'There you are, my dear,' he exclaimed, just as though he hadn't seen her at breakfast. 'Had a pleasant day? Alice has gone with friends down to Brighton—she needed a breath of sea air. She'll be back some time this evening. Something smells good...'

'Beef casserole, Father. Would you like it straight away?'

'Yes, yes, why not? And we must have a little chat. I'm sure you have enough money to keep us going for the time being? I find myself short of cash...'

Araminta sat down opposite him. 'No, Father, I haven't. I've paid some of the bills which were owing. Did you know how many there were? And there is no money left.' She crossed her fingers behind her back as she uttered the fib.

Her father blustered. 'Well, I must say that's very shabby of you, Araminta. Heaven knows how I struggle to keep you girls in comfort and pay our way.'

'Yes, Father, I'm sure you do. If Alice could find a small job, she could spend her money on clothes and outings and that would leave a great deal more housekeeping and you wouldn't need to worry.'

'You're hard, Araminta. I'm sorry to say it, but you
lack a loving understanding. Alice and I are all the family
you have—you should feel proud that you can help us
to make life tolerable.'

Araminta cleared away the plates and fetched the
pudding. There was no point in saying anything, for her
father wasn't going to listen. If I could save a little
money, she thought wildly, I could leave home and find
a job—anything to start with—and then get a training
for something worthwhile.

Her father eyed her across the table. 'You look
thoughtful, Araminta. I hope it is because you realise
the sorrow your selfishness causes me.'

'Father, you sound like someone in a Victorian novel.
Have some more pudding?'

'Thank you, no. Sufficient must be left for Alice; she
will probably be hungry after such a long day.' He got
up from the table and stalked from the room, leaving
her to clear the dishes and wash up. She stood at the
sink, looking out of the window at the evening sky filled
with scudding clouds through which the moon was doing
its best to shine, and for no reason at all she started to
think about Professor Lister again. He would be home
by now, she reflected, sitting beside the fire with Goldie
and Neptune crouched beside him. He would be wearing
his reading-glasses and be deep in some interesting book,
and presently Buller would come in to tell him that dinner
was served ...

The professor was indeed in his drawing-room, sitting,
exactly as Araminta had imagined, beside his hearth,
the dogs sprawled over his feet, a book in his hand. Only
he wasn't reading; he was, if only she had known it,
thinking of her. He was vaguely irritated that he seemed

unable to get her out of his mind—after all, there was no reason why she should keep popping up in his thoughts. She was a very ordinary girl, hired to do a job which she had done with skill, and that was the end of it. On the other hand he had found her an ideal companion, making no effort to entertain him, making sensible conversation and with the gift of being silent— restfully so, without fidgeting or combing her hair, powdering her nose or fussing with lipstick. She wasn't a girl to demand attention either, but she was perfectly capable of holding her own in a no-nonsense fashion.

He got out of his chair as Buller appeared in the doorway. In a few days, when he had an hour or so to spare, he might look her up to see how she was getting on. The suspicion that she wasn't happy at home crossed his mind, and he frowned; it would be interesting to see her sister again and meet her father...

Araminta, optimistic by nature, arrived at Mrs Taylor's house exactly on time to be admitted by Mrs Loder.

'Back again, ducks. Plenty of work for you this morning.' She chuckled. 'Someone gave the old lady a box of chocs—she ate the lot.'

Araminta braced her small person and went into Mrs Price's room, pulled the curtains back and turned to survey the dire results of the chocolates. Mrs Price, her nightdress and the bed were liberally coated. Mrs Taylor would tear her cleverly tinted hair out by the roots when she saw the mess, although if Mrs Loder had told her about it she would quite likely, and very prudently, defer her visit until everything was cleaned up.

Araminta led the chocolate-covered old lady to the cloak room and washed her from top to toe, helped her to dress, and set her in a chair before tackling the bed.

There was no help for it, it would have to be clean sheets again...

Mrs Taylor came during the morning, and by that time Araminta had the room and its occupant in a more or less clean state. Mrs Price, settled in her chair, had given endless orders and directions in a querulous voice, which Araminta had allowed to flow over her head while she bundled up sheets and pillow-cases. Mrs Taylor greeted her parent and then stopped short.

'Miss Smith, not another change of sheets, I hope.'

'Somebody gave Mrs Price a box of chocolates,' said Araminta and, since Mrs Taylor gave her an unbelieving look, she spread out a sheet for her inspection.

Mrs Taylor averted her eyes. 'Kindly take everything through to the kitchen. Someone will have to see to it.'

But not me, said Araminta silently, returning presently with Mrs Price's morning drink.

Mrs Taylor was still there. 'Really, I don't know what is to be done,' she declared.

'No more chocolates,' offered Araminta, and received a cutting glance. She ignored that. 'If someone were here while Mrs Price has her meals?' she suggested.

'Impossible. I have a very busy life.' Mrs Taylor narrowed her eyes. 'You could stay until one o'clock and see that my mother has her lunch.'

'I'm afraid I can't do that, Mrs Taylor. The arrangement was for three hours each morning.'

She waited for Mrs Taylor to say that in that case she would get someone else, but she didn't. All she said was, 'See that the fire is kept up—the room's not warm enough.' She glanced round. 'There is a window open.'

'Fresh air,' explained Araminta politely. 'The room wasn't smelling very nice when I got here.'

She wondered then who had brought the old lady's breakfast; surely they would have seen the mess? It didn't seem prudent to ask.

Mrs Taylor went away then and didn't come back until almost half-past twelve. Perhaps this was how it would be each day, thought Araminta, making good her escape.

The days dragged themselves to the end of the week: hard-working mornings and the chores to see to when she got home, for if Alice was there it was seldom, and then she would be sulking because Araminta didn't dare to let her do the shopping. Their heads were just above water, but only just; there was no knowing what Alice would see and buy if she had any money with her. And her father, sitting opposite her at supper each evening, darted reproachful glances at her and, when he caught her eye, smiled wistfully.

On Friday evening he was more cheerful. 'It's Saturday tomorrow—pay-day,' he said happily.

Araminta chose to misunderstand him. 'Father, didn't they pay your cheque in last week? Have you given the housekeeping to Alice?'

'Well, my dear, there were one or two bills—gas and electricity—and Alice needed one or two things. I quite forgot to let you have any money. You shall have it next week. I daresay you'll get paid from the agency tomorrow—you can use that, can't you? I'll pay you back.'

'I'm sorry to disappoint you, Father,' said Araminta, 'but Mrs Taylor doesn't intend to pay any fees until I'm not needed there. I believe there's a cousin coming to stay who'll take over from me, but I don't know when.'

Mr Smith was indignant. 'But that's absurd; you're entitled to your money each week. Still, I dare say there's still something left over from that other job of yours.'

He smiled at her. 'I'm sure you've got something tucked away for a rainy day, my dear.'

It was no use, she thought wearily; she loved her father, despite the fact that he allowed money to trickle through his fingers like sand through a sieve. When her mother had been alive it hadn't been as bad, but now that Alice was grown up, wanting things...

'I've almost no money, Father,' she said gently, 'but I'll do the best I can. Perhaps you can persuade Alice to find a job—she won't listen to me...'

'Well, understandably, Araminta. You have hurt her feelings, you know—she's such a sensitive girl.'

At least it's Sunday tomorrow, thought Araminta as she dressed the next morning. She wondered what happened to Mrs Price on that day and what kind of a mess she would find on Monday morning. But first, Saturday.

Old Mrs Price was in a bad mood; she had never shown a sunny disposition but this morning she was more irascible than ever, and on top of that Mrs Taylor was coldly angry because Araminta regretted that she wouldn't be able to come on Sunday morning. 'The agency arranged for me to come from Monday until Saturday,' she pointed out quietly.

'Oh, I know that, but what are a couple of hours to you? You'll still have the rest of the day to yourself. I've a luncheon party I simply cannot miss.'

'Perhaps if you ring the agency, they will have someone who could take over tomorrow?' suggested Araminta.

'Don't be ridiculous, Miss Smith. Who would want to work on a Sunday?'

Who indeed? reflected Araminta.

'I shall be late back, I've things to do,' snapped Mrs Taylor. 'You'll have to wait until I return.'

'I will wait until half-past twelve, Mrs Taylor,' Araminta said reasonably, 'but then I shall go, for I have things to do. Indeed, I hoped to leave at noon today— that was the arrangement.'

'I shall replace you as soon as possible.' Mrs Taylor flounced away and presently left the house.

The morning was much as the other mornings had been. Mrs Price was cross and contrived to do everything twice as slowly as usual; the fire wouldn't burn briskly and the old lady spilt her elevenses all over the floor. Araminta mopped up and prayed for the morning to end.

Which it did, eventually, and, better than that, Mrs Taylor was only fifteen minutes late. 'Don't expect to get paid until you leave,' snapped Mrs Taylor. 'And mind you're here on Monday morning.'

Araminta nipped smartly through the door before Mrs Taylor could think of anything more unpleasant to say, took a breath of more or less fresh air and stood still on the pavement. Drawn up to the kerb was a dark grey Rolls Royce with Professor Lister sitting in it. He got out when he saw her, opened the door on the other side, scooped her neatly on to the seat and got in again. All without a word.

'Well, really,' said Araminta, at a loss for words. A silly remark, but she couldn't think of anything else.

He turned to look at her. 'Hello, Miss Smith—have you had a trying morning?' He sounded concerned, and she supposed that her appearance justified his enquiry.

'I have had a trying week,' she told him. 'Are you visiting a patient, Professor?'

'No. I thought we might have lunch together?'

'How did you know where I was?'

'I rang the agency.'

He began to drive away and she said quickly, 'It's kind of you to ask me to lunch, but I really should go home.'

'Why?'

'Well, there is the shopping to do, and if Father and Alice are at home they will expect lunch.'

'They won't worry if you are late back?'

'Worry? No, of course not, they'll think that I've had to stay at Mrs Taylor's for some reason or other.'

'That's all right, then. We can talk over lunch.'

'I'm not dressed for lunch,' said Araminta and pointed out in the most matter-of-fact way that she was very untidy.

'In that case we will go somewhere where you can tidy yourself and eat in quiet surroundings.'

'Why do you want to see me?' asked Araminta. 'If it's another job, I'm supposed to stay with Mrs Taylor until someone comes to take over.'

'That is easily remedied. As to why I want to see you, we will discuss that presently.'

He turned his head and smiled at her, and her heart gave a little skip of delight. She told herself sharply that that was quite enough of that; to get ideas about him would never do. She said primly, 'Very well, Professor,' and sat quietly until he turned into the forecourt of St Pancras station and parked the car.

She got out when he opened her door, and gave him a questioning look.

'We'll go to the restaurant, and then you can go and do whatever you need to do and join me there.'

The restaurant was large and, strangely enough, quiet. He led her to a table in a corner, said, 'Off you go, you know where I am,' and took out his reading-glasses to study the menu.

If I were looking for romance, I certainly wouldn't find it with Professor Lister, reflected Araminta, doing things to her face and repinning her abundant hair. Nothing could improve the cotton sweater and skirt under her jacket. It struck her then that that was why he had brought her here for lunch; she looked like hundreds of other women travelling to and from work, and had no need to worry about her appearance. The idea sent a little glow of pleasure through her person, that he should have thought of that and spared her any embarrassment.

He got up as she joined him. 'What would you like to drink? Sherry?'

'You can't drink, can you,' she asked him, 'since you're driving? So I won't either. I'd like a tonic water and lemon with ice.'

He ordered for her and picked up his menu. 'I don't know what the food's like, but choose whatever you would like.'

'A mushroom omelette and a salad, please.' And when he had ordered that, with a steak for himself, she said, 'You wanted to talk about something?'

He smiled a little, took off his glasses and put them in his pocket. 'Ah, yes, but might that wait until we have had our lunch? I should like you to tell me about this job of yours—from the look of you, I think it must not suit you.'

She went red and put her hands, roughened by a week of rendering Mrs Price and her room clean, in her lap, out of sight. If he noticed, he said nothing, but merely sat there, waiting for her to speak. She began carefully, 'Well, it is rather—well—messy, and Mrs Taylor...' She launched into an account of her work, careful not to exaggerate, and contrived to finish quite cheerfully. 'I don't expect I'll have to be there much longer, there's someone—a cousin, I think—coming to look after Mrs Price. The next job may be very much better.'

The waitress brought their lunch and the professor made no comment, but talked about a variety of subjects which only needed the briefest of replies. She ate her omelette with appetite, accepted his offer of apple-pie for dessert and, since he seemed to have lost all interest in her work, took care to follow his lead and talk about nothing much.

It was over coffee that he observed in his calm way, 'Of course you cannot go back to that dreadful woman. I'll see the agency and arrange for you to leave as from today.'

Araminta looked at him, aghast. 'Oh, please don't do that. I... We need the money...' She could have bitten her tongue the next instant for making such a revealing remark. 'What I mean is...' she began.

'I am aware of what you mean, Araminta.'

Diverted, she exclaimed, 'You called me Araminta.'

'And I hope I shall continue to do so,' he observed blandly. 'Now, I want you to listen to me, and pray do not interrupt.'

'Well, I'll try not to.' She poured their coffee and handed him a cup. 'But I might, you know, if you surprise or annoy me.'

'I may surprise you, but I hope that I shall not annoy you.'

Araminta took a sip of coffee. She was nicely full, the coffee was excellent, and she had to admit that she was very much enjoying the professor's company. She wondered briefly what he wanted to say to her, but, before she could begin to guess, he said in a conversational tone, 'I have decided to take a wife. Until recently I have found my life quite satisfactory; I have my work, my friends and a pleasant home, but I must admit I feel the need for a companion, a good friend, someone to come home to and who will listen to how my day has gone. I suppose that, like most men, I have hoped that one day I would meet a woman I would want to love and live with for the rest of my life, but it seems she has eluded me, so I must settle for second-best. After all, many love-matches come to grief, whereas a marriage founded on friendship and compatibility may well prove very successful.' He paused to look at her, sitting very much at her ease, smiling a little.

'Why are you telling me this?'

'I considered it right to explain my feelings before I ask you to marry me, Araminta.' She put her cup down very carefully in its saucer, and he added, 'I've surprised you, Araminta, but not, I hope, annoyed you.'

'Yes, you have, but I'm not annoyed. No one has ever asked me to marry them before; it's not something any girl would get annoyed about.'

She reflected that something had annoyed her, though; she was to be second-best, was she? If—and the idea was laughable, of course—she should marry him, she would make him eat those words, even if it took years. It was, in fact, a good reason for marrying him . . .

A fleeting vision of the professor kneeling at her feet begging forgiveness flashed through her head and was instantly sternly repulsed. She was aware that he was studying her face intently, and she met his gaze without coyness.

'I am serious,' he told her.

'Yes, I know that. You don't know anything about me.'

'I know all that is necessary; the rest I can learn later, can I not? But you are what I would hope to find in a wife, Araminta.'

She said honestly, 'Yes, maybe, but you don't love me, do you?'

'No, but I like to be with you. You are restful, and reasonable too; I believe that you could cope with being a medical man's wife very well—the late meals, the sudden calls away from home, the hours I like to spend in my study. All I ask of you is that, I think, for the time being at least, there need be no talk of love. Liking can grow into affection, and that is important in marriage.'

Araminta saw no point in contradicting him. Love, she considered, was what mattered in marriage—if you loved someone you put up with anything, just to be with him.

'I do not expect you to give me your answer now, only when you are ready. You may wish to talk it over with your father.'

She shook her head. 'No. I think not. You see, they would like to have me stay at home and keep house and look after things. When I have made up my mind, I'll tell him and Alice.'

He nodded. 'We will go to the agency and I will arrange for you to be replaced. Whether you decide to marry me or not, I cannot allow you to stay there with those unpleasant people.'

'But I——' she began, to be interrupted gently.

'No, Araminta, I must insist on it. Should you decide not to marry me, then I will see to it that you have more suitable work—away from home, if you prefer.'

She asked curiously, 'How will you do that?'

'I know very many people, and there are many possibilities for you.' He smiled gently. 'But I hope very much that you will consent to marry me.'

He signalled for the bill, and they went out into the station and then to the car. 'First the agency, and then I will take you home.' And, at her questioning look, 'No, I won't come in and meet your father, not until I have your answer.'

At the agency Araminta had to admit that the professor had impressive powers of persuasion. He had the austere owner agreeing to everything he said within ten minutes, he extracted the week's money from her, assured her that if ever he needed her assistance in finding an employee he would certainly call upon her, and ushered Araminta out of the bare little office, ignoring the sly glances she cast at them both. Araminta hadn't noticed; she had too much to think about.

He drove her home then, got out to open her door, and then got in the car again. She poked her head through the open window, inches from his face. 'Thank you for my lovely lunch, and thank you for proposing to me. Shall I write and let you know?'

He put a hand over hers where it clutched the window. 'How long will it take you to make up your mind?'

She thought for a minute. 'If I think about it for the rest of today and all tomorrow...'

'May I come and see you tomorrow evening? Whatever the answer is, we can have a meal together and discuss your future.'

'Very well, but I don't want to tell Father and Alice until it's settled.'

'I understand.'

She withdrew her head and watched him drive away.

There was no one at home; a note lay on the kitchen table asking her to do the shopping for the weekend. It was in Alice's handwriting but her father had added a PS: 'Sorry there's no money—but get everything put on account.'

There was no need for that; she bought what was necessary and wondered about the following week. If she married the professor, how would they manage at home? Alice would have to get a job, and what could she do? And even if she didn't marry him, she had no work for the following week. Would she be marrying him to escape from home and all its petty worries, or because she really wanted to be his wife?

She made a pot of tea then and thought about it. It was a pity there was no one to advise her. She thought with longing of her mother, a woman of strong character, who had passed on her good sense and plain face to Araminta, kept a guiding hand on the purse-strings and taken care that her husband didn't spoil Alice. There wasn't anyone... Yes, there was. She went to church on Sundays and the vicar of St John's was elderly, gentle and, she thought, wise. Her mind made up to go and see him the next day, she got on with preparing the supper; her father and Alice would be hungry when they got home.

Beyond remarking that she had been late coming home, they asked no questions; they only asked if she had done the shopping, fell to discussing the film Alice had been to see, and then switched on the television until it was time for bed.

In the morning Araminta took herself off to church and, after the service, lingered until she could speak to the Reverend Mr Thorn.

'If you could spare ten minutes?' she asked him. 'I need some advice.'

He led the way back into the church and they sat in one of the pews, and, conscious that he would be expected home for his dinner very shortly, she laid her problem before him in as few words as possible.

When she had finished, he asked simply, 'Do you love this man, Araminta?'

'No, but I like him very much. I like being with him, I'm easy with him and there are things we both like—I mean serious things. He's a serious man. I don't think he has asked me to marry him without thinking a great deal about it first.' She thought for a bit. 'I should like to marry him and I think we would be happy, even though we don't love each other. Is that possible?'

'Oh, yes, mutual trust and respect and liking would develop in time into true affection. You are concerned for your father and sister?'

She nodded. 'They aren't very good with money— since Mother died I've looked after them and the house.'

'Perhaps it would be a good thing if they were to take that responsibility upon themselves. Once they have got over the shock of fending for the two of them, it might open up an entirely new way of life.' He sat silently for a while and then said, 'I think you should marry this man. It is natural that he should want a wife and he has chosen you, and from the sound of him he seems a man who would not take decisions lightly.' They both got up and he took her hand. 'If and when you make up your mind, remember that you must keep to it steadfastly, Araminta.' He smiled. 'Now go home and dish up the lunch and let me know...'

CHAPTER SIX

'WHY are you so late?' Alice wanted to know crossly. 'It's a good thing it's steak and kidney pudding, for I've no intention of cooking the dinner. It's something I hate doing.'

Their father, coming into the kitchen added, 'It would have been kind to have warned us that you would be so late, my dear.'

It seemed hardly the moment to tell them her news.

She decided that it was some kind of sign that neither her father nor Alice intended to go out that afternoon. They would be at home when the professor came, and she was thankful for that; she would never convince them that she was going to get married without some evidence. She got the tea a little earlier than usual and wondered when he would come. She was a sensible girl, but her nerves were positively jangling.

They didn't have to jangle for long, though; just after six o'clock the Rolls stopped before the house and the professor gave the doorknocker a resounding thump.

'The door, Araminta,' called Alice from her seat in front of the television. Her father, immersed in the Sunday papers, didn't look up.

Araminta went to open the door and the professor stood on the doorstep, looking down at her, wondering in his calm way if he was making the biggest mistake of his life. On the whole, he thought not; Araminta's ordinary face was lifted to his and held an expression which reassured him. She had beautiful eyes, he reflected, and a gentle mouth. He smiled then. 'Am I too early?'

She stood aside to let him come in. 'No. Do you want to know now?'

He smiled at her. 'Yes, please.'

'You haven't changed your mind?' She was quite serious. 'I mean, it's quite all right if you have—no harm done.'

'No, I haven't changed my mind, Araminta.' He bent and kissed her cheek. 'Shall we tell your father?'

She nodded. 'He'll be annoyed...'

He appeared unmoved at the idea. 'We will go back home presently and lay our plans.' He took her hand and went with her into the sitting-room.

Less than an hour later, sitting beside Jason in the car, Araminta relived the rather unpleasant half-hour with her father and Alice. They had stared in surprise as she and Jason had entered the room, and Alice had jumped to her feet. 'What a lovely surprise,' she had cried. 'I always hoped we'd meet again. Have you got another job for Araminta? Is that why you're here?'

Araminta had said quickly, 'Father, this is Professor Lister—my father, Jason.' She had seen Alice's look of surprise and her quick frown, and clutched his hand harder. It had been given a reassuring squeeze before the professor had shaken hands with her father.

'Araminta and I have a surprise for you, sir. We are to be married shortly.'

Her father had been too surprised to speak for a moment; it was Alice who had said, 'Marry Araminta? But that's ridiculous—I mean, she doesn't know how to dress decently, she's not even pretty, you'll be ashamed of her...'

She had stopped then because the look on the professor's face had frightened her. He had spoken very quietly. 'I'm sure you don't mean that, Alice.' He had turned to her father. 'I'm taking Araminta back with me now so that we can discuss the wedding. I have arranged for her to leave Mrs Taylor. I am sure you will be delighted at our news.'

Araminta had felt sorry for her father: he had looked as though he had been hit on the head and wasn't sure what was happening. He had said slowly, 'We shall have to manage as best as we can without you, Araminta,' a remark which had made her feel guilty, as he had intended.

But the professor had said briskly, 'I'm sure Alice will become as good a housewife as Araminta.'

Then he had suggested that Araminta should go and get her coat. She had no idea what had been said while she was upstairs, but she had a nasty feeling that when she got back that evening she would be met with reproaches and perhaps worse. But that was still hours away; she peeped at Jason and saw that he was smiling a little. She said, 'I'm sorry Father wasn't... That is, it was a great surprise to him.'

He gave her a quick sidelong glance. 'Yes, I could see that. Would you rather not go back home this evening, Araminta?'

'I expect when they've talked it over it will be all right, thank you.'

His grunt reassured her in some way.

When they reached his house she wondered what he had told Buller, for Mrs Buller came into the hall and she and Buller both wished her happy and shook the professor's hand with delighted smiles. When Mrs Buller had gone back to her kitchen and Buller had taken their coats and gone away too, Araminta asked, 'How did they know?'

He took her arm and urged her into the drawing-room. 'I told Buller that if we were here by eight o'clock he and Mrs Buller could congratulate me and wish you well.'

He sat her down, fended off the dogs, and sat in his chair opposite her, and after a few minutes Goldie and Neptune settled at his feet. It wasn't until Buller had come in with champagne in a silver bucket and gone soft-footed away that the professor said, 'I have a very full week ahead of me—if you would agree, we might decide upon a date for our wedding this evening.' He opened the champagne and handed her a glass. 'To you, Araminta.'

'To us both,' said Araminta. 'I'll marry you whenever you want me to, but I don't know anything about you— only that you are a surgeon and live here.'

He laughed. 'Supposing we get married first and take our time to get to know each other later? I don't want you to be at home for longer than is necessary. I'll get a special licence and we can be married as quickly as possible. Have you any preference? Your local vicar?'

'Yes, please. I asked his advice and he told me to marry you—he said that mutual liking and respect were important and a foundation for...for...'

'Affection,' said the professor gently. 'He's quite right. Good. I'll arrange everything and let you know. Your father and sister will come?'

She gave him a troubled look. 'Perhaps they won't. Perhaps it might be better if we just got married—just the two of us.' She added, in a matter-of-fact voice which hid unease, 'I haven't anything suitable to wear—I hope you won't mind?'

'You will still be Araminta even in a potato-sack. You always look very nice.' He watched her as he spoke, aware that he might hurt her—the last thing he wanted to do. He sensed that she would refuse to take money from him until she was his wife, but he was aware that wedding clothes were important to a woman; after all, he had two sisters who had married with all the pomp expected of them. He would have to think of something. 'I don't think it matters, do you?' he asked. 'We shall be just the two of us...'

'As long as you don't mind.'

Over dinner they discussed the wedding with the impersonal interest of two people talking about a ceremony between mutual acquaintances. It was to be as soon as the professor could get the licence and arrange time in which to get married. 'I know it should be the bride who decides the day, but I shall have to rearrange my work so that I am free. I should like to see you as much as possible—may I ring you each day so that we can meet? You will be at home?' He saw her hesitate, and added quickly, 'You are thinking of taking another job—please don't. For one thing, this licence may take less time than I anticipate.'

'All right, I won't. Do you have a lot of friends? They might not like me.'

He smiled a little. 'When we are married you shall go shopping and buy some spectacular outfits and burst upon them in a blaze of high fashion. You will be a great success with my friends, Araminta.'

He began to talk about his sisters and then his work; casual remarks, some of which she stored away to think about later. As they sat by the fire presently, drinking coffee from paper-thin cups, she reflected that she must be out of her mind; how in heaven's name had she ever

agreed to marry this rather remote man about whom she
knew almost nothing? She could, of course, change her
mind, and she knew without any doubt that he would
accept her decision calmly. Only of course she had no
intention of doing that; she had given her word. Besides, she liked him. She looked across at him and found
his eyes upon her, and blushed, for all the world as if
she had spoken her thoughts out loud.

She blurted out, 'I hope I'll be able to fit into your
life, Jason.'

'I have no doubt of it. You may even find it rather
dull. I suspect that you will be visited by my colleagues'
wives and invited to join various committees and meet
to gossip over coffee. Will you like that?'

'If that's what your wife is expected to do, then I'll
like it.'

'I've a cottage in north Essex—we'll go there for the
weekend and take the dogs. You like the country?'

'Yes—oh yes, I do. Is there a garden?'

'Quite a large one. There's a nice old man who comes
from the village and keeps it in trim when I'm not there.
His daughter keeps the place clean and cooks, though I
daresay we could manage the meals between us.'

'It sounds heavenly.' She saw the time and said, 'I
think I'd better go home. It's been a lovely evening. I'm
still not sure if I'm dreaming.'

He drove her home then, getting out of the car and
waiting until she had gone inside before driving away.
She had asked him hesitatingly if he would like to go in
with her, but except for a glimmer of light in the hall
there was no sign of life. They had agreed that, since it
was almost midnight, her father and sister would already
be in bed. 'I'll come tomorrow evening,' he assured her.
'Your father will be home then.'

Neither her father nor Alice was in bed; they were waiting for her in the sitting-room.

'I have been very disturbed by your news, Araminta,' began her father. 'This Professor Lister—who is he? How long have you known him? Will he be able to offer you the kind of life to which you are accustomed?'

Araminta sat down. Her father was talking like someone in a Victorian novel again. She said in her sensible way, 'No, it won't be at all the same, Father. He has a very nice home, and I shan't have to go out to work or do the washing-up or the ironing. I have known him for some time now; we saw a lot of each other while I was at Tisbury.' Which wasn't quite true, but it might allay any fears her father might have. She thought it unlikely that he had any fears about her anyway.

'You're sly,' said Alice in a furious voice, 'going behind our backs, leaving us in the lurch. How are we going to manage, I'd like to know?'

'Well, there'll only be two instead of three for a start, and if you get a job you'll manage very well. After all, Father has quite a good salary. A part-time job will give you as much money as I earned; you can spend it on clothes and whatever you want; there'll be ample housekeeping then.'

'Don't think I'm coming to your wedding,' Alice raged. 'You've nothing to wear anyway—I suppose it'll be some hole-and-corner affair.'

'No,' said Araminta, 'just very quiet. Jason doesn't have much leisure.'

Her father shook his head. 'Well, you're old enough to know your own mind, Araminta. I only hope you're not making a big mistake.'

Araminta got up. 'Don't either of you want me to be happy?' she asked.

'Why should you have all the luck?' Alice asked angrily. 'You needn't come crawling home when he sees what a mistake he's made.'

'And you, Father?'

Mr Smith shook his head. 'Naturally I hope that you will be happy, my dear, but I doubt it. You're out of his class, for a start. He'll probably be ashamed of you among all his lofty friends.'

Araminta, accustomed to looking on the bright side of things, nevertheless cried herself to sleep. But, beyond a slightly pink nose, in the morning there was no sign of that. She cooked breakfast as usual, replied suitably to her father's comments about the weather and the busy day he had ahead of him, and wished him goodbye in her normal quiet fashion. He had barely answered her and she supposed that, while she was still at home and not working, he would present the same injured expression on his face. It was therefore a great surprise to her when he came home at his usual time and came into the kitchen where she was getting their supper.

He said in a warm voice, 'I'll come to your wedding, Araminta. I'll give you away, if you would like that.' He fished in his pocket. 'I daresay you would like a new dress.'

He put some notes on the table. 'It's the best I can do.'

'Father—how kind of you. I'd love a dress to wear, and I had hoped that you would come to our wedding. Thank you very much. I hope you haven't had to borrow——'

He said hastily, 'No, no. A small overdraft which I can settle next month. Where is Alice?'

'She went out about an hour ago, but she'll be back for supper.' Araminta came round the table and kissed her father's cheek. 'Father, it is most kind of you and I'm so grateful.'

He shrugged his shoulders. 'Must make an effort. Is the fire lighted in the sitting-room? I'll run through the paper while you're getting supper.'

He went and sat down in his chair and picked up the paper, but he didn't read it. He felt smug and pleased with himself, as though it were his money he had given to Araminta and not Professor Lister's—sent to him by special messenger, together with a courteous letter requesting his presence at his daughter's wedding. It had been more than the hundred pounds he had given to her, but Alice had just as much right to it as Araminta. It should have been his pretty Alice who was marrying a well-to-do man; what had Araminta ever done to deserve such an assured future?

He was immersed in the news when the phone rang.

Araminta lifted the receiver, and the professor's voice wished her good evening, said he would be with her in half an hour and that they would go back to his house for dinner. His goodbye was brief.

Araminta put the cottage pie in the oven and went to tell her father. 'Supper will be ready in about half an hour. I expect Alice will be back by then.'

Her father lowered his newspaper. 'I suppose we must expect this until you leave us. We'll manage, I dare say— I've had a hard day's work...'

'But Alice hasn't,' said Araminta with a snap, and then contritely, 'Sorry, I didn't mean that, but it would make things much easier if she would tackle the housekeeping.'

Her father didn't answer, and she went to her room and got into her suit, did her face and her hair, and was waiting when the Rolls came to a quiet halt before the door.

She answered the professor's thump at once and said, 'Hello,' then, 'Would you like to come in?'

She was surprised when he smiled and said, 'Yes,' but she led him into the sitting-room and sat quietly while the two men exchanged small-talk. It was as Jason got up to go that he observed, 'You will be giving Araminta away, of course, Mr Smith?'

'Of course. It is too early to fix a date, I suppose?'

'We will let you know as soon as it is arranged.' He put a hand on Araminta's arm. 'Shall we go, my dear? We have a good deal to discuss still.'

He swept her out of the house and into the car, where Goldie and Neptune were mounting guard from the back seat. 'I shall have the licence in a few days,' Jason told her as he eased the car into the evening traffic. 'I'm rather heavily booked for the next few weeks—would you mind very much if we marry at a moment's notice? You will come back with me to our home but you may not see much of me for a few days. We could wait, of course, but I want you out of your father's house as soon as possible. What have they been saying to you to make you cry?'

'I haven't...' she began, and started again; if they were to have a good marriage, telling lies wouldn't be a good start. 'I thought it didn't show. Father and Alice are upset because I won't be there...'

'To work and clean and cook for the pair of them. I do not mean to be unjust, Araminta, but they are rapidly turning you into a doormat. You deserve better than that. I don't promise you an exciting life, but I shall do my best to make you happy.'

'Yes, I know. Father said that we're not in the same class and he's right, you know.'

'If you're going to talk like that, I shall beat you,' said the professor placidly, so that she laughed, suddenly at ease and happy.

Over Mrs Buller's delicious dinner—orange and tomato soup, then cassoulet of duckling followed by syllabub—Araminta told Jason of the unexpected gift her father had given her. 'Now I can buy a dress,' she told him happily, 'and he said he would give me away, although last night he said he wouldn't come to the wedding.'

'Now that is good news indeed,' agreed the professor, suitably surprised, while he wondered silently how much of the money he had sent Mr Smith had been held back from Araminta. Just as soon as he could, he would arrange for her to go shopping and buy anything and everything she wanted.

They went into the drawing-room for their coffee and sat by the fire talking like old friends, and when there was a phone call from the hospital asking him to go there urgently, she made no demur but agreed to be driven back by Buller.

'I do hope you won't have to stay up half the night,' she told him, 'and do take care how you go, won't you?'

He dropped a kiss on her cheek and went away. Really, he had chosen well, he reflected. Araminta would fit into his life very well—the kind of wife he had wished for, reflecting his moods, a quiet and intelligent companion. He smiled; it was most agreeable to be told to take care, and for someone to mind if he was kept out of his bed for half the night.

Buller drove Araminta back presently and waited until she entered the silent house. He had asked her if she drove a car as they went through the city. 'The professor will see that you have lessons, miss. You could manage this Rover easily, even here in London. It would be handy if you could drive yourself, him being away so much.'

She had agreed pleasantly; she liked Buller and his wife. It was a contented household, run on oiled wheels. For a moment she wondered what she was going to do with her days. Of course, learning to drive would keep her busy for several weeks, and there were the dogs to walk, and in the evenings there would be Jason...

The supper dishes had been left by the sink. She took off her jacket, tied an apron round her small waist, and turned on the taps. While she washed up, she thought about how she would spend her hundred pounds.

She spent every penny of it the following day, leaving home soon after breakfast while Alice was still strolling around in the kitchen in her dressing-gown, and for the next few hours she went slowly along Oxford Street, comparing prices, deciding what she could afford. She saw quickly enough that a hundred pounds wasn't going to go far; an elegant little suit with a boxy jacket and a pleated skirt left her with thirty pounds, which she laid out on a pretty blouse and plain court shoes—cheap, but a good imitation of more expensive footwear. Since she had some money over from the job at Mrs Taylor's, she browsed through the undies department of a large store and bought a modicum of lacy trifles, feeling guilty since the money could have been spent on meals for the rest of the week. She was walking down Oxford Street, feeling pleased with her purchases, when she stopped to look in a hat-shop window. Her suit was a dark green and burgundy plaid with a little velvet collar, and the hat in one corner of the window was exactly the right colour of burgundy. Moreover, it was marked half-price.

Araminta bought it; it sat charmingly on her neat head—
not a white tulle wedding veil, but the next best thing...

She bore her purchases home and found Alice lying
on the sofa.

'You're back,' said Alice in a wispy voice. 'I feel
rotten—you'll have to get the supper. I'd like a cup of
tea and some lunch...'

Araminta put down her parcels and went to look at
her sister. She looked the same as usual, only rather more
cross. 'It's a bit late for lunch,' she pointed out. 'I'm
going to make myself a cup of tea. I haven't had lunch
either—I'll make toast.'

She went up to her room with her purchases and
stowed them away in the bottom of the wardrobe; tonight, when she went to bed, she would try everything
on. Now she went down to the kitchen, made tea and a
plate of buttered toast and took the tray into the sitting-
room.

'I'll have it here,' said Alice peevishly.

'Why not?' agreed Araminta cheerfully, as she poured
tea for herself and began on the toast.

Alice watched her for a few moments. 'What about
me?' she asked.

'I've made enough toast for both of us,' said
Araminta. 'Alice, dear, I think you must stop pretending that you're not strong, that you can't get a job
like everyone else. I'm sure you'd enjoy it once you got
started. Think of the money!'

Alice got off the sofa and started on the toast. 'Why
should I, when Father lets me buy what I want? It's all
very well for you to talk. You'll live like a lady while
I'm stuck here...'

'If you had a job you'd meet people.'

Alice took the last piece of toast and poured her tea. 'You're such a prig. You'll see, he'll get fed up with you in no time at all—you're plain and dull and your clothes are awful. I shall laugh myself sick.' She burst into easy tears. 'You always took such care of me, I never had to do anything.'

'That was because I thought you were ill. But you're as well as I am, love, and you surely don't want to sit about for the rest of your life?'

Alice tossed her head. 'I don't—I've plenty of friends—we have a grand time.' She went back to the sofa and lolled back on it. 'I hope there's something decent for supper.'

Araminta went to the kitchen, disappointed that Alice hadn't wanted to see what she had bought. She was at the sink with the taps running when the telephone rang. She didn't hear it, nor did she hear Alice answering it.

'She's not here. I don't know where she is—out for the evening, I dare say.'

She had slammed down the phone before the professor could reply.

Jason had got home earlier than he had expected and, rather to his own surprise, the first thing he had done was to telephone Araminta. A quiet evening over dinner and then an hour's talk would be pleasant. He replaced the receiver unhurriedly. He didn't believe Alice; if Araminta had been going out, she would have left a message. He whistled to the dogs, shrugged on his coat and went out to his car.

'I'm going to fetch Miss Smith,' he told Buller. 'I dare say we'll be back within the hour.'

The rush-hour wasn't quite over; it took him some time to reach her home, and it was already dusk when he got out of the car and banged the knocker.

Araminta came to the door, her gentle mouth curling into a delighted smile. She said, 'Hello, Jason,' and waited for him to speak.

'Get your coat,' he told her. 'We'll go back home for dinner—we still have a lot to say to each other, haven't we?' His smile was so kind that she felt the urge to burst into tears and bury her head on his shoulder.

'Come in,' she invited. 'I won't be a minute. I didn't expect you.'

'Telephoned half an hour ago and was told you'd gone out, probably for the evening.'

'Oh! Oh, dear. I was in the kitchen. I expect Alice...' She looked up at him worriedly. 'So sorry...'

'Run and get your coat, my dear, and stop apologising for your sister.'

'Yes... Well, would you like to go into the sitting-room?'

He shook his head. 'Just fetch your coat; you can do whatever else you want to do when we get back.' He bent suddenly and kissed her, and she flew upstairs with the delightful feeling that perhaps she wasn't as dull and plain as Alice had said.

Coming down again, she poked her head round the sitting-room door. Alice had the television on and Araminta raised her calm voice above the din. 'I'm going out, Alice. Supper's ready to cook.'

She whisked herself out again before Alice had answered.

'She's a bit cross,' she explained as they drove away. 'I'm sure she didn't mean to mislead you.'

To which remark Jason made no reply.

It was during dinner that he told her that he would
have to go to Birmingham on the following day. 'I shall
spend the night there and, if all goes well, get back some
time during the next day. I'll ring you tomorrow evening
around nine o'clock and let you know. Oh, and we may
marry on Saturday. Will you see your Mr Thorn
tomorrow? It's very short notice, but I dare say he can
fit us in. I'll come for you on Thursday evening and
we'll go and see him together, shall we?'

'Yes, very well, Jason.' She spoke in her usual sensible way, but her insides felt peculiar, as though she had
taken a step that wasn't there; it was almost panic. . .

The professor, watching her without appearing to do
so, said comfortably, 'Now tell me what you've been
doing with yourself all day.'

It seemed a perfectly normal thing to do—to tell him
about the suit she had found and the perfectly matching
hat that so luckily was half-price.

'I look forward to seeing it,' he told her. 'Pack your
things on Friday, will you? I'll collect them in the
evening.'

'I've not got very much,' she told him seriously. 'Two
cases—they'll go in the boot?'

He assured her that they would.

The evening was as pleasant as the previous ones had
been. It was surprising, she reflected, how completely at
ease she felt with him; it was as though she had known
him all her life. The thought of not seeing him on the
following day made her feel quite sad, but at least she
would have things to do—pack her things and go and
see Mr Thorn. Jason didn't try to delay her when she
said after an hour or so that she would like to go home,
but he drove her back, saw her into the house and drove
off again.

She went to see Mr Thorn the next morning. 'A wise decision,' he told her. 'I believe that you will make the marriage a success, Araminta, and be a good wife. I should like to have met Professor Lister before you marry.'

'Tomorrow evening,' Araminta told him. 'He's in Birmingham today and doesn't get back until tomorrow, but he'll come in the evening. May we come and see you then?'

'Of course. The ceremony is to be a quiet one?'

'Just us. Father says he will give me away. Could it be some time in the morning?'

'You are going away afterwards?'

'No. No, I don't think so. Jason's not free. I was thinking of Father—he wants to take Alice out for lunch. Could it be about half-past ten or eleven o'clock?'

'You will be having a family lunch?'

'No,' she said soberly, 'Alice isn't coming to the wedding. Just Jason's registrar and your wife—we have to have two witnesses, don't we?'

'Shall we say half-past ten?' Mr Thorn's voice was gentle. 'Then, if the professor is free, you will have the rest of the day together.'

She did the shopping next, since Alice had dressed and gone out early and declared that she didn't know when she would be back, then went home and tidied the house and, after a sandwich and coffee, went to her room and began to pack. She had nothing suitable for an eminent professor's wife to wear, she reflected. She hoped he wouldn't feel ashamed of her, and she supposed that he would give her some money to get the right kind of clothes. She hoped he would think of that, for she didn't think she could ask him. She might have to, she thought; he hadn't struck her as being very observant. She was, of course, quite mistaken.

It was quite early in the afternoon of the next day when the professor arrived. Alice was out again, and Araminta was on the point of washing her hair. She opened the door at his knock.

'You're back,' she observed. 'How nice. Did all go well? Come in, do. I was going to wash my hair...'

He smiled down at the pleased face. 'We're going out first. Wedding-rings—I had almost forgotten.' He bent and kissed her cheek. 'Get a coat and we'll go now.'

'I can't go like this.' She looked down at her tweed skirt and woolly jumper. 'Would you wait for five minutes? I'll be quick.'

'Five minutes then.' He strolled into the sitting-room and stood looking out of the window at the street. As soon as he could spare the time, he would take her to the cottage...

He took her to a Bond Street jeweller and waited patiently while she tried on various rings, choosing in the end a plain gold band, and when they were alone for a minute he said, 'Will you give me a ring, Araminta? You can pay for it out of your allowance later on.'

'Oh, yes, please. I thought of it, but I haven't any money. If you don't mind lending it to me...'

'Not in the least. I am, after all, going to endow you with all my worldly goods on Saturday.'

So she chose a ring for him too, as plain as hers. As they left the shop, he said, 'I have to go back to my consulting-rooms in an hour or so, but there's time for tea.'

He took her to a small and elegant tea-room and gave her Earl Grey tea and delicious cream cakes, and watched her ordinary face glow with pleasure. He didn't care for tea-rooms himself, but it was rather like taking a child out for a treat and he felt unexpected pleasure from that.

He drove her back presently, waiting only until she had let herself into the house before driving away for his appointment. 'I'll be here as near seven o'clock as I can manage, and we'll go home for dinner afterwards,' he told her.

Alice was at home, in the sitting-room doing her nails. She looked up as Araminta went in. 'You're back—what's for supper?' And when Araminta told her, she said, 'You'll see to it, won't you? I don't feel like cooking.'

'I'll get everything ready, but I'm going to see Mr Thorn at seven o'clock and I won't be back until later this evening.'

'Then Father will have to take me out. I don't feel up to cooking.'

Araminta, on her way out of the room, turned to ask, 'Alice, are you going to find a job? If you did, you could afford to pay someone to do the housework once a week.'

Alice shrugged her shoulders. 'I might think about it, I suppose. It won't be any of your business anyway, will it?'

Araminta, in the kitchen making a fish pie, clashed the saucepans and their lids in an attempt to work off her ill-humour. It was fully dispelled at the sight of the professor, though. Pausing only to wish her father a pleasant good evening and warn Alice that the pie was in the oven, she skipped through the door and into the Rolls. It was surprising, she reflected, how quickly one could become accustomed to the good things in life.

Mr Thorn liked the professor, she could see that at once. They sat in the comfortable shabby sitting-room at the Vicarage and drank the coffee his wife offered them, and the two men discussed the chances of England against Australia during the next tour. It surprised her that Jason knew so much about cricket. The actual arrangements about the wedding were disposed of in no time at all; indeed, while they were being discussed, the professor's manner was that of a man who was talking of someone else's marriage, not his own.

'That's settled,' he observed placidly as they got into the car. 'We'll have dinner, shall we?' He gave her a sideways glance. 'Cold feet?'

'Certainly not,' said Araminta, who had.

Not for long, however; the evening was as comfortable as the previous ones had been. Curled up in her bed later that night, she thought sleepily that the future was everything she could wish for.

She hadn't expected flowers in the church when she arrived with her father, but there they were: glowing bunches on either side of the altar and a wrought-iron stand of roses and lilies and carnations near the pulpit, and there was a little posy of lilies of the valley and rosebuds for her—the vicar's wife had handed it to her in the porch, and then followed them into the church. Jason was there; for one dreadful moment she had imagined that he hadn't come, but there he was, enormous and calm, his best man, his registrar, beside him. She tucked her hand in her father's arm and walked steadily down the aisle.

CHAPTER SEVEN

As ANY girl would, Araminta had dreamed of bridal veils and white satin and bridesmaids, but now none of these mattered. Mr Thorn had a splendid voice; the words of the service rolled off his tongue in all their splendour and she listened to every one of them, standing beside Jason, small and straight in her new suit, making her responses in a steady voice.

The service was quite short; they went out of the church arm in arm and her father and the best man came behind them with the vicar and his wife, and in the porch they stood for a few minutes, being congratulated. The professor was quite at his ease, his hand holding Araminta's in a secure clasp. He didn't let it go when her father said, 'Well, I'll be off. I'm taking Alice out to lunch—mustn't be late.' He pecked Araminta on the cheek and went away with a brief word to Jason, who wished him goodbye with a bland face which gave away nothing of his feelings.

'You'll come back for half an hour and drink to our health?' he asked Mr Thorn. 'Peter will wait while you take off your cassock, Vicar, and bring you and Mrs Thorn to our house.' He smiled down at Araminta. 'We'll go on ahead, my dear.'

He popped her into the car and drove away, beginning at once on a casual rambling conversation so that Araminta, who had suddenly found herself tongue-tied, began to feel normal again.

'I like the outfit,' said Jason. 'You look very nice, Araminta. You have good taste in clothes. Next week you shall go shopping and, if I can spare the time, I'll come with you.'

'I'd like that, for I've no idea what to buy.'

'I find that remark, coming from a woman, very hard to swallow.' He gave her a brief smile. 'I can see that I'll have to lend a hand.'

The Bullers were waiting in the hall, beaming their congratulations, while the dogs pranced around getting in everyone's way.

'I should have carried you over the threshold,' observed the professor. 'I quite forgot. Remind me to do so at some time.'

They had gone into the drawing-room and there was no time to talk, for a moment later the others arrived and Buller came in with champagne and a tray of tiny smoked salmon sandwiches. The talk was cheerful and of nothing much, and Araminta, drinking her second glass of champagne, thought how delightful it was among these friendly people who seemed to like her. The future, considerably enhanced by the champagne, bade fair to be rosy, and presently, when everyone had gone, they would spend a pleasant day together; there was a great deal she had to learn about Jason—his likes and dislikes, his work, what he liked to eat, how he spent his leisure...

Their guests went and they had lunch together, a festive meal at which Mrs Buller had excelled herself. They talked comfortably about the wedding, and he told her about Peter, his registrar, and a little—a very little—of his work at the hospital. Not just one hospital: he went wherever he was needed, frequently abroad.

Araminta sat quietly, not interrupting, listening carefully, storing away odds and ends of information. Later, she hoped, he would tell her about his family. After lunch, perhaps, since they had the rest of the day together.

She was to be disappointed; over their coffee he suggested that she might like to see her room and go with Mrs Buller round the house. 'I've some phoning I must do—I'll be in my study.'

So she went with Mrs Buller up the stairs and into a large room, furnished in a cunning mixture of pastel colours which showed the beautiful mahogany bed and dressing-table to the best advantage. There were little easy chairs and a *chaise-longue*, delicate bedside tables with porcelain lamp-stands and a vast tallboy. The clothes-cupboard along one wall was vast too; she could never fill it, she reflected, peering into the bathroom, and then, with Mrs Buller sailing in front of her, through another door into another bedroom, smaller, and furnished without any of the delicate colours and lovely fabrics of her own room.

'The professor's room,' said Mrs Buller. 'Well, his dressing-room, as one might say, ma'am.'

Araminta, momentarily diverted at being called 'ma'am', wasn't really listening.

They toured the house right up to the top floor, where the Bullers had their small flat, and it was all quite perfect. 'Would you wish to unpack now, ma'am, or shall I show you downstairs?'

'Oh, downstairs, please, Mrs Buller. I haven't much to unpack.'

The small sitting-room behind the dining-room was not grand like the drawing-room but very comfortable, with small Regency furniture and two high-backed armchairs, one each side of the fireplace. It would be nice to have tea there, thought Araminta, one each side of the fireplace like the married couple they now were, while Jason told her about his day...

There was another room too, a small library, with shelves of books and leather chairs beside the centre table. Araminta drew a blissful sigh and went back to the drawing-room.

There was no one there, but presently Buller brought in the tea-tray. 'Shall I let the professor know, ma'am?' he asked.

She jumped up. 'I'll go, thank you, Buller.' She tapped on the study door and was answered by a grunt. When she went in, Jason looked at her over his spectacles as though he had never seen her before. She faltered for a moment, then asked, 'Would you like your tea here?'

'Is it already that time? No, no, I'll join you.' His smile reassured her; she must have imagined that look of complete indifference...

They had their tea, making comfortable conversation the while, and later they had dinner together and it seemed to Araminta as though they had known each other for ever, talking at their ease, lapsing into silence without the feeling that there was need to talk.

It was while they were drinking their coffee that the phone rang. Buller answered it. 'The hospital, sir,' he said from the door, 'in your study.'

The professor went unhurriedly and didn't come back for several minutes, and when he did it was to tell her that he was needed urgently. 'I expect to be gone for some time,' he told her. 'I'll say goodnight now and see you at breakfast. Sleep well!'

Araminta reminded herself that she was a surgeon's wife now, and that this was the way it would be for the rest of her life: she would be shut out of the greater part of his life. She wasn't even sure if he wanted her to know about it. He had said that he wished for someone to be at home when he got there at the end of the day, but he had told her to go to bed. The pleasant picture she had had in her head of waiting up for him with a hot drink and a sympathetic ear she now dismissed as sentimental nonsense. She finished her coffee and, with Goldie and Neptune keeping her company, she embarked on a slow tour of the portraits and pictures on the drawing-room walls. Family, she supposed, and ancestors, some delightful miniatures, and a group of pencil sketches of a child's head. She wondered if they were of Jason, and fell to wondering about him as a small boy. Perhaps, when she got to know his sisters, she would be able to find out.

Since by eleven o'clock there was no sign of Jason, she went to bed. She fell asleep at once, waking in the small hours, her head very clear as it so often was at that time. Jason had married her for companionship, for someone to come home to. He had been honest about that: love wasn't going to enter into it, although later perhaps his liking might develop into affection. So she would be a good companion. She went back to sleep.

He was reading some papers when she got down in the morning, but put them down as she went into the dining-room, asked if she had slept well and if she had all she wanted.

'Like a log,' she told him cheerfully. 'How about you? Were you kept at the hospital?' An unnecessary question—she could see he was tired. 'It was something urgent? I do hope you were able to sort it out.'

They had sat down at the table and Araminta poured his coffee as Buller came in with several covered dishes. The professor got up, asked her if she would like eggs and bacon, scrambled eggs or boiled, served her and then himself, and sat down again. 'Yes, I hope the man will recover,' he told her, 'but shall I not put you off your breakfast if I talk about it?'

'I'll tell you when to stop,' she suggested, and began on her scrambled eggs.

She listened intelligently, although she didn't understand all that he was saying, and she did not interrupt; it was obvious to her that he was mulling over his night's work—thinking out loud, getting it off his chest. When he finished she said, 'It must be very satisfying to be a surgeon, to be able to do something when everyone else just has to stand around feeling helpless.'

'I quite often feel helpless, Araminta.'

'Well, yes, I can understand that, but you still go on doing your best, don't you? Will you be able to go to bed now for a few hours?'

She passed the toast-rack and poured him more coffee.

'No, I'm afraid not. I must go back to the hospital, but I should be home by six o'clock. I'll give myself a morning off in a few days and we'll go shopping.' He smiled. 'At least, you will shop. I shall sit on one of those uncomfortable little gilt chairs and admire what you buy.'

He got up, gathering his papers. 'And before you argue about it, I wish my wife to have everything she wants, within reason. We can't possibly buy all you need in one morning, but we can make a start.'

He dropped a friendly hand on her shoulder as he passed her chair.

'Shall I walk Neptune and Goldie in the park?' she asked.

'Would you? Buller will tell you where he usually goes. We might take them again this evening before dinner.'

He had gone, leaving her to sit at the table, wondering what to do with the greater part of her day.

The problem was solved for her within a few minutes. Buller, coming in to clear, enquired of her in a fatherly manner if she would care to step into the kitchen and have a little talk with Mrs Buller. 'You'll be wanting to know how the house is run, ma'am—the shopping and so on—and you'll wish to inspect the household linen.'

So Araminta went along to the kitchen and sat down at the scrubbed table and paid attention to Mrs Buller's motherly titbits of information. She would, it appeared, be expected to see Mrs Buller each morning to discuss the day's meals with her. As to shopping, Fortnum & Mason delivered a weekly order, which she would make out, but there were, naturally, items needed from time to time which she might care to purchase for herself. The household expenses were handed to the professor at the end of each month, but no doubt he would be glad if those could be dealt with by ma'am.

Mrs Buller beamed across the table. 'If you've the time to spare, ma'am, we might take a look at the cupboards, and if you want anything altered I'd be happy to oblige.'

'Mrs Buller,' said Araminta earnestly, 'please don't alter anything. I'm sure the professor likes the way his home is run by you and Buller. I know very little about running a house such as this one; I've always done the housework and cooking and my home was small. I'll have to learn a great deal from you and I hope you will help me.'

'Don't you worry, ma'am, me and Buller will do all we can to make things easy for you. You'll soon find your feet—such a nice young lady as you are, you can't fail to get into the way of it. Now, shall we check the linen-cupboards first? You'll be wanting to take the dogs out presently—we might go through the china and the silver in the pantry when you come back before lunch.'

'That sounds fine.' Araminta got to her feet and they went upstairs to a vast cupboard at the end of a passage leading from the landing, and spent the next hour examining damask tablecloths, napkins by the dozen, piles of linen sheets and pillow-cases, blankets as soft and light as thistledown, and satin-covered quilts.

Mrs Buller answered her unspoken thought. 'The professor's parents lived here; his mother bought only the best.' She chuckled. 'I doubt if he knows the half of what's here. It's a pleasure to check everything with you, ma'am. Men just don't want to know.'

When they got back downstairs Buller had coffee waiting, and stayed a moment to offer advice as to the best way to get to the park. 'And I was to remind you to keep to the main paths, ma'am. The dogs are obedient, they'll come when you call them. They like a good run.'

It was a blustery day. Araminta found her way easily enough and, once in the park, let the dogs loose for half an hour. They rushed around happily, coming back to her every so often and racing away again. They came at once when she called, to her secret relief, and they walked briskly back home to find Buller waiting to dry paws and lead the dogs away for the biscuit they were allowed before settling down in front of the drawing-room fire.

As for Araminta, she was served a delicious lunch in the cosy room at the back of the hall and, still feeling like a guest in the house, she joined Goldie and Neptune by the fire to read the newspapers and then, wishing to know something of Jason's world, to search the book-shelves for something which might give her an insight into it.

She was struggling to understand a heavy tome on haematology when Buller brought in the tea, and she still had her nose buried in it when Jason came home.

He greeted her cheerfully, refused tea, and took a look at the book. She answered his raised eyebrows rather tartly. 'Well, I have to begin somewhere...'

He sat down in his chair and the dogs fell on his feet. 'Of course you do,' he agreed placidly. 'I'm delighted that you're interested. Will you allow me to choose the books which will teach you quickly and easily?'

She nodded, and he asked, 'What exactly do you want to know?'

'I want to be able to understand when you tell me things—the names of operations and illnesses, what goes on in hospitals, what sort of anaesthetics are used, the different treatments...'

'Supposing you start with the hospital? The different departments, the operating theatres, the intensive care unit, Casualty. I'll bring some books with me tomorrow, and when you have read them I'll take you round so that you can see everything for yourself. Then you can work your way through the basics.'

'Thank you. It's so that I can understand a bit... You don't mind?'

'Of course not. I'm delighted. Now tell me, what have you done with your day?'

She told him, and then asked him about his.

He told her briefly and added, 'What about that walk? I could do with some fresh air.'

She got her coat and, with the dogs on their leads, went with him up to the park. It was a chilly evening and the wind was still blustery. They walked briskly, Araminta skipping a few steps now and then in order to keep up, and as they walked they talked—about nothing much and with comfortable silences from time to time. They might have been an old married couple, thought Araminta, peeping at his calm face. This must be how it would be when one had been married for half a lifetime or more, walking companionably together, not having to make conversation, at ease with each other. Was that being in love? she wondered. In that case, was she in love with Jason? If so, it wasn't in the least as she had imagined it would be. Where were the excitement and the thrill, the galloping pulse, the caught breaths? But she liked him; she liked him very much.

They went back presently and, after a pleasant dinner, Jason excused himself and went away to his study, taking the dogs with him. Araminta, struggling once more with haematology, decided to find the nearest wool-shop in the morning and buy wool and knitting-needles and the most complicated pattern she could find.

She gave up her reading presently and sat thinking about her father and Alice. They knew where she lived now and she had given them her phone number, and she had half expected to hear from her father. She would wait a few days, she decided, and then go and see them. Jason had told her that she was to have an allowance; she could give some of it to Alice...

There was no sign of Jason, so presently she went to bed, not sure if he would expect her still to be there when he eventually came back into the drawing-room.

It was past midnight when he came into the room, opened the doors for the dogs, and stood looking out at the quiet garden. He was still mulling over the lecture he was to give on the following day and, to tell the truth, he had forgotten Araminta.

However, he felt pleasure at the sight of her at the breakfast-table in the morning, smiling and cheerful and as neat as a new pin. 'I've rather a busy day,' he told her, 'a lecture this afternoon to first-year students and one or two things to clear up afterwards. I'll probably be home rather later than usual.'

'I'll ask Mrs Buller to get dinner—when? Eight o'clock? We'll have something that won't spoil, so it won't matter when you come home.'

'Will you do that? I'll phone if I get held up.' He got up to go. 'I've given myself the morning off tomorrow; we'll do that shopping.'

She conferred with Mrs Buller after he had gone. 'He'll be tired,' said that lady. 'A nice fricassee of chicken and one of my cheese soufflés—he'll need to sit a while with a drink—and what about a nice queen of puddings to follow?'

'That sounds ideal, Mrs Buller. Do you want me to do any shopping? I'll take the dogs first, but there will be plenty of time after that.'

'There's a few good shops ten minutes' walk away, ma'am. Buller will show you where. I could do with some fresh thyme and marjoram and basil, if there is any. There's a good greengrocer there—sells good fresh stuff.'

So Araminta took herself off after walking the dogs, carefully primed as to how she should go by Buller. It was pleasant walking through the quiet streets lined with dignified houses, and the shops, when she reached them, tucked away discreetly down a narrow lane, were de-lightful: the greengrocer, a delicatessen, a very up-market newsagent, a chic boutique and, right at the end, a tiny shop selling wools and embroidery silks.

She had a little money in her purse. She went in and poked around under the friendly eye of the elderly owner. She had intended to buy wool and needles; instead she purchased a fine canvas with a complicated pattern of flowers suitable for a chair-seat or a firescreen. She bought the silks to work it, reflecting that she need never sit idle again.

'You'll need a frame,' said the elderly lady; she found one and demonstrated how to stretch the canvas taut between the hoops.

Araminta bore her parcel away, bought the herbs, and then loitered outside the boutique. There wasn't much in its small window, but she coveted everything there. Tomorrow, she reminded herself, she was to go shopping; she had no idea what Jason would want her to buy, but certainly she would need more clothes if she were to go anywhere with him. The wedding outfit was all right but it wouldn't do for his wife; she had the good sense to know that.

She spent the afternoon getting started on the embroidery. She had never done tapestry before, but she was handy with her needle and not impatient. After tea she told Buller that she would take the dogs into the park, since otherwise they would have to wait until Jason came home, which might be late.

'The professor wouldn't wish you to go into the park alone in the evening.' Buller was deferentially fatherly. 'They will be quite happy in the garden, ma'am, and if the professor is late home, I will exercise them myself.'

So she went upstairs and changed her blouse, her only possible concession to dressing for the evening, and when she came downstairs Buller told her that the professor had telephoned to say that he would be kept late at the hospital. 'Eight o'clock at the earliest, ma'am, and what would you wish Mrs Buller to do?'

'Would she mind keeping dinner back? I'm sure the professor will be hungry. And please have your own meal at the usual time—I don't know when that is, but it's only just gone six o'clock.'

He replied suitably and went back to the kitchen, where he told his wife that the new missus was a very nice young lady. 'Very thoughtful,' he added. 'She'll suit the professor a treat. Won't get in the way of his work...'

Mrs Buller looked thoughtful and said nothing.

When the professor got home just after eight o'clock, Araminta greeted him without fuss. 'Would you like ten minutes or so before dinner, or are you ravenous?'

'Ravenous, but I'd like ten minutes first.'

'Well, sit down. I'll get you a whisky.' Which she did without waiting for his answer.

When she took it to him he said, 'I believe that I have been missing something before I took a wife.'

She smiled and went to sit down again. He wouldn't want to talk, she could see that. He was tired; perhaps after he had had a meal he would tell her about his day.

However, although he talked of this and that while they ate, he didn't speak of his work, and afterwards he whistled to the dogs, told her he would take them for a quick run, and left the house. She went back to the drawing-room, having agreed pleasantly, and presently, when he came back, he sat in his chair with the dogs beside him and, after a few casual remarks, put on his glasses and buried his handsome nose in the day's newspapers.

Araminta stitched busily, her thoughts just as busy. Did she bore him? He had said that he enjoyed her company, that he liked her, but was that enough to satisfy him? Would he have been happier married to a girl who expected to be entertained, talked to, admired, someone to break down his self-contained way of life? Perhaps I have made a colossal mistake, she reflected, and, for all I know, he's discovered that too. She looked up and found his eyes on her.

'You must not think that because I sit here with my nose buried in the newspapers that I am not aware and content to have you sitting there like a friendly mouse. You are filling an empty space in my life, and I think that when we have had time to get to know each other, we shall have a successful marriage.' He smiled. 'You agree, I hope?'

'Yes, I do,' she told him; anything else she might have said was cut short by the phone. It was a lengthy conversation, mostly yeses and noes on his part, and then a stream of instructions of which she understood very little. He went back to his reading then, and she sat for another half-hour or so, and then wished him a quiet goodnight and took herself off to bed.

He got up when she did and opened the door for her, touching her shoulder briefly as she went past him. 'Sleep well,' he said very kindly.

He hadn't said any more about their morning shopping, she thought as she got ready for bed. Perhaps he had forgotten about it, and she hadn't liked to remind him. She counted the money in her purse—there was almost nothing in it—and she wondered what she should do. Her clothes were quite inadequate but he didn't seem to be aware of that, and to ask him for money was something she couldn't do. She lay wakeful for a time until she decided with her usual good sense that worrying wouldn't help in the least; she might as well go to sleep. Which she did.

At breakfast he asked her if she had any preference as to which shops they should go to.

'Oh, we're going...?'

He stared at her. 'Of course—did I not say so?'

'Yes, yes, you did, but I thought that you might be too busy.' And, as he still looked at her with questioning eyebrows, 'I don't know about shops. I mean, I've always gone to Marks & Spencer or C & A, and just once or twice when there's been a sale to Country Casuals.'

He said smoothly, 'Then I think it had better be Harrods. I imagine there will be plenty of choice there.'

She said on an excited breath, 'What do you want me to buy?'

He was carefully casual. 'Oh, everything. Outdoor clothes, dresses—you will get drawn into the consultants' wives' coffee-mornings and tea-parties—something for the evenings. I'm not very socially minded but I do have several close friends...'

Araminta's eyes had grown round, her head already agreeably filled with the picture of new clothes. 'Will you please tell me how much I may spend?'

'I can't do that, for I don't know what you intend to buy. You shall choose what you like, and if it costs too much I'll say so.'

'Promise?'

'Promise.'

On their way up to the first floor of Harrods Jason observed, 'You'll need things for the country—we'll go to the cottage next weekend. Get a Burberry.'

It was hard to know where to start, but once the saleswoman had grasped the fact that madam needed an entire wardrobe and that her husband was there, sitting on one of the fragile chairs, apparently agreeable to the entire shop-floor being purchased if his wife wished, there was neither let nor hindrance. Before an hour was out Araminta had acquired a tweed coat and skirt, two knitted suits, a short jacket, a number of pleated skirts with the necessary blouses and sweaters, a Burberry, and several pretty dresses. She had tried everything on and stood before Jason for his approval and, once or twice when the saleswoman wasn't there, had hissed at him in an urgent tone that he was spending an awful lot of money.

He had only smiled a little and told her to leave that to him. Bearing this remark in mind, she allowed the saleswoman to lead her to the footwear department, where she bought boots, several pairs of wildly expensive shoes, and stockings to match. Back again with the professor, she was reminded that she would need a hat for church, so she was whisked away to look at hats and, since she couldn't decide between a felt with a brim, which seemed to do miracles for her profile, and a jaunty little velvet affair, she had them both.

They were well into the second hour now, and she remembered that Jason had said that he had some patients in the afternoon. She sat down beside him, her cheeks pink, her eyes sparkling. 'I've bought simply masses of clothes. I expect you want to go home—it's almost lunchtime and you have patients later.'

He smiled a little. 'I'm glad you have found what you liked. I think that tomorrow you must come and get the rest.'

'Oh, undies? Well, yes, I would like some new things, but I could go to——'

He cut her short. 'No, will you come here, Araminta? I have an account and you will get everything you want. You might see a couple of frocks to wear when we dine out...'

She nodded wordlessly. She hadn't dared to look at any of the price-tags, but he must have spent a great deal of money. The clothes were good, though; she consoled herself with the thought that they would last for a long time.

The saleswoman came with the bill and he paid with a credit card, asked for everything to be delivered to his home, and swept Araminta out of the shop and into a taxi. He was a man who did things without fuss, she reflected: a lifted finger, a nod, and the doorman had a taxi at the kerb within moments.

Back in the house, sitting down to lunch, she tried to thank him. 'I hope you don't think that I married you for money,' she said worriedly, 'because I didn't.'

'I know that, Araminta. You married me, did you not, for the same reasons as my own: friendship, pleasure in each other's company, a mutual liking? What is mine is now yours also, my dear.'

He left the house presently, with the warning that he might not be back until six o'clock. She longed to ask him where he was going after he had seen his patients—the hospital, she supposed. She wished once again that she knew more of his life. Patience, she told herself, there was plenty of time.

The Harrods van arrived then and Buller bore the boxes up to her room and she set about unpacking them. She tried everything on again, fearful that it would look different away from the luxurious showrooms, but the clothes looked even better, she decided, and hung everything away in the closet. Tomorrow she would buy undies . . .

After her solitary tea, with the dogs for company, she went back to her room and showered and got into one of the pretty dresses—nut-brown crêpe-de-Chine with a wide Quaker collar and cuffs of cream silk—and it became her very well. Pleased with her appearance, she went down to the drawing-room and sat down to work at her tapestry, and while she sat there she tried to decide what to do about her father and Alice. Did they want nothing more to do with her? she wondered. Should she go and see them, or wait and see if they phoned or wrote to her? She would ask Jason's advice when he got home.

He came presently, and she went into the hall to meet him. He said, 'Hello,' briskly, and then added, 'I've some work to do before dinner—you won't mind?'

Her 'Of course not' was uttered in her usual sensible way, but she wondered what he would have said if she had told him that she did mind. 'You're a busy man's wife,' she muttered, going to sit by the fire again. Perhaps it would be better if she didn't go to meet him in the evenings when he got home? That way, if he wanted to go at once to his study, he could do so without having to apologise. She picked up the tapestry and stitched busily, concentrating on the pattern, and presently Buller came to ask whether dinner was to be served at the usual time, or would the professor wish for a later hour?

'I'll go and see,' said Araminta. She tapped on the study door and went in in answer to his quiet 'Come'. He was at his desk, his glasses on his nose, a book in his hand. Just as he had previously done, he looked at her as though he was surprised to see her there. Indeed, she had the impression that he wasn't really looking at her; his thoughts were miles away.

'Dinner,' she said briskly. 'Mrs Buller would like to know when you would like it—it can easily be put back for a while.'

He took off his glasses. 'No need. I had rather forgotten the time.' His finger was marking the page in his book, and he withdrew it reluctantly. He glanced at his watch. 'I've five minutes? I'll be with you.' He got up to open the door for her. 'Make that ten—time for a quick drink.'

He spent the rest of the evening with her, talking about the cottage, telling her where it was, and then suggesting that as soon as he could manage it they might go to Tisbury and see how Lydia was getting on. 'And you must meet Marjorie,' he told her. 'I believe she intends to give a dinner party so that you can meet as many people as possible.'

Araminta said placidly, 'That will be nice,' and inwardly quailed at the prospect. She would have liked to ask about visiting her father and Alice, but Jason had picked up the medical journal from the table beside him and was leafing through it. She tidied away her work, said cheerfully, 'I'm quite tired after such an exciting day. Goodnight, Jason, and thank you for all my lovely clothes.'

Surely that might remind him to look at her and see the new dress? It didn't. He got up and went to the door with her, wishing her goodnight, smiling as she passed him, and going back to his chair to immerse himself in a long article concerning jaundice in the new-born.

As for Araminta, she gained her room, hung the dress in the closet and got ready for bed, all the while weeping quietly. She wasn't sure why; she only knew that she felt sad about something and unhappy.

It was silly to cry for no reason, she told herself sharply. She had had a lovely morning and tomorrow she would go shopping again; she had more clothes now than she had had in her entire grown-up life, so what had she to cry about?

She went to the windows and pulled back the curtains and looked out on to the garden below. It was very quiet at the back of the house; it might almost be country. As she looked, the outside light by the French windows of the drawing-room was switched on and the dogs, followed by the professor, came into the garden. The dogs raced off into the dimness beyond the circle of light, but he stood in its brightness, his hands in his pockets, looking up at the sky. She stared down at him, knowing now why she was crying. She had fallen in love with him. Perhaps it had happened weeks ago, when they first met, and she hadn't known it, only that she liked to be with him. So love wasn't always like a bolt from the blue; it could come gradually as well, sneaking up on one without warning. Now this was a pretty kettle of fish, since he had shown no sign of even a mild romantic thought about her.

The obvious answer was to get him to fall in love with her. Araminta, a practical girl and used to making the best of things, took one last loving look at the professor and jumped into bed, fired with the laudable purpose of doing just that. On the face of things it seemed unlikely, but with patience, and the help of a good hairdresser and products from the cosmetic counter at Harrods, and never forgetting to present him with a cheerful friendly manner with no hint of romance, she could at least have a good try.

CHAPTER EIGHT

ARAMINTA went down to breakfast the next morning wearing one of the new skirts, a silk blouse and a cashmere cardigan. The blouse and skirt were sand-colour, the cardigan duck-egg blue, and she had put on a pair of Italian shoes. Very suitable, she considered, turning this way and that before the enormous looking-glass behind the clothes-closet door. Perhaps Jason would notice...

He did indeed look up as she went into the room. He took off his glasses too, put down the letter he was reading and stood up with a pleasant, 'Good morning, Araminta,' but as soon as she sat, he resumed his own seat, gave her an absent-minded smile and picked up his letter.

Buller, hovering, murmured, 'Bacon and egg, ma'am, or perhaps a poached egg?'

She shook her head; she would have choked on either, but, since Buller was looking worried, she took a piece of toast and nibbled at it and poured herself a cup of coffee. Buller went away and she filled Jason's cup too and, since he had finished his letter, enquired if he would be home late or not.

'Round teatime, if I'm lucky. We'll take the dogs for a run. There's a letter for us both from Marjorie—she wants us to go over for dinner on Friday. There will be one or two friends there—a chance for you to meet them.'

She agreed quietly and, seizing the opportunity, asked, 'Jason, would you mind if I phoned Father? I'm not

sure... That is, they may not want to have anything to
do with me just at the moment, but perhaps once they're
used to me being married to you...'

'You'd like to go and see them? Or have them here,
by all means.'

She said awkwardly, 'I don't want them to think that
I'm—I'm flaunting being married to you, if you see what
I mean.'

He was putting his spectacles away in his pocket and
didn't look at her. 'Yes, I see what you mean, Araminta.
Perhaps it would be best if you phoned—that would give
you some idea of how they feel.' He gathered up his
papers and presently left the house.

She went to the kitchen for her morning's chat with
Mrs Buller and, that done, went into the park with the
dogs. After lunch she put on her new suede jacket and
took herself off to Harrods. She felt a little uncertain
without Jason; supposing they queried her right to charge
everything to his account?

She need not have worried. Wandering around looking
for underwear, she encountered yesterday's saleswoman, who, when Araminta confided her doubts, assured her that there was no problem and took it upon
herself to take her to the lingerie department and hand
her over to a friendly young woman who produced a
tempting collection of silk and lace garments. Araminta,
shocked at their price but carried away with their sheer
prettiness, allowed herself to be coaxed into buying
nighties to go with them and a pink quilted dressing-
gown with matching slippers. She hadn't looked at their
price-tags; Jason had told her not to, hadn't he? She
consoled herself with the thought that everything she
had bought was so well-made and of such fine materials
that she would be able to wear them for years. She went

back the way she had come, and her friendly sales-woman stopped her to suggest that she might like to see a couple of dresses which had just come in that morning.

That reminded Araminta that they were to dine with Jason's sister. Perhaps a suitable dress? 'Something right for a dinner party?' she asked, and was shown the very thing: pale grey chiffon over a pink slip, its full sleeves gathered into satin cuffs, the modest neckline bordered with the same satin. Standing before the mirror, Araminta saw that it suited her very well. 'The thing is,' she explained, 'I'm not sure if it's long skirts...'

'No problem, madam—if you would prefer a short dress, then bring this one back and we will exchange it.'

The matter happily settled, Araminta took herself home again to have her tea in the sitting-room she found so cosy, the dogs beside her. The professor, coming home earlier than he had anticipated, found her there, her nose buried in a medical journal.

Her heart gave a happy leap at the sight of him, but she said sedately, 'You're home early—how nice. Would you like tea?'

'I had tea with Theatre Sister. Shall we take the dogs for their run?'

She got up at once. 'I'll fetch a coat...'

'Have you phoned your father?'

'No. Not yet.' She paused at the door, looking up at him. 'But I will.'

'Shall we do it now?' he suggested quietly, and picked up the phone on a side-table, dialled the number and handed the phone to her.

Her father answered.

'It's Araminta,' she told him, and flinched at his 'Tired of being a rich man's wife already, my dear? Just my joke. We're getting along very nicely. I could do with a small loan if you can spare it. Mustn't forget your old father, must you?'

Before she could answer, Alice's voice cut in. 'He's not tired of you yet? Early days, I suppose. Don't come back here, we're doing very nicely. Maybe I'll come and visit you one day.' She hung up, and Araminta put the receiver down slowly.

'They don't want to see you, but they expect you to send them money,' said the professor.

'Yes—how did you know?'

'My dear, I have met your father and sister. You have been a dutiful daughter and sister, and they're banking on that.'

'You make me sound a prig.'

'No, no, never that. Don't send them any money, Araminta, I'll deal with that side of things. I may be able to help your father in some way. Will you leave it to me?'

'You're kind. You have enough to do without bothering with my family.'

He put an arm round her shoulders. 'Allow me to be the best judge of that.'

They walked for an hour in the park with the dogs, comfortable in each other's company. Araminta could have walked forever, but they went back presently and dined in a leisurely fashion before the professor went to his study, leaving her to her needlework. This, she perceived, was to be the pattern of their evenings when they were at home—but not forever. Something must be done about that.

She went back to Harrods the next morning and had her hair washed and trimmed and dressed in an artful knot which made the most of its gentle brown. She had a manicure too. A facial was unnecessary, she was told; her skin was perfect, her eyebrows silky arches, her lashes long and curling. A little discreet lipstick, mascara of a suitable colour to enhance the lashes were all that was needed. She went back home well pleased with the beautician's efforts and hoped that she would be able to cope with the hair...

The professor, coming home rather later than usual, paused in the doorway to look at her. She was wearing the same pretty dress she had so hopefully worn after they had gone shopping together, and this time he noticed it. There was something different about Araminta too. He had always found her pleasant to look at but now he took a second look, uncertain what the difference was.

As she put down her work and got up to greet him, he said, 'That's a pretty dress...'

It wasn't much, but it was a start...

The following evening, getting ready for Marjorie's dinner party, Araminta paused to look in the looking-glass. She would never be pretty, but it was surprising what powder and lipstick and a professional hair-do did for one. She had worried over the right dress, but now, studying herself, she decided that she had made the right choice. The pink silk gleamed faintly through the grey chiffon and the dress was a perfect fit. As for the shoes—she had never had anything so elegant in her life before: grey satin with high, slender heels. She collected the evening bag which went with them, picked up the gossamer wool wrap and went downstairs.

Jason was in the drawing-room, standing by the open doors to the garden, watching the dogs romping together.

He turned to look at her as she went in, and she thought how magnificent he looked in his dinner-jacket.

'Charming,' he told her in a voice which, to her anxious ears, sounded merely friendly, 'and will you wear these with it? A belated wedding-gift.'

Pearl drop ear-rings set in diamonds. 'They're beautiful,' she exclaimed. 'Thank you, Jason.' She crossed to the big mirror over the fireplace and hooked them in and stood admiring them.

'This too,' said the professor. 'I should have given it to you before we married, but it slipped my mind.'

He slipped the ring over her wedding-ring: sapphires ringed with diamonds and set in gold.

'Oh,' said Araminta, and then added, 'It fits...'

'I remembered the size when we bought the wedding-rings.'

She stretched up and kissed his cheek. 'Thank you, Jason. I'll take great care of it and wear it constantly.' Were her efforts paying off already? She doubted it. She wondered if any other girl had been given an engagement-ring with the observation that it had slipped the giver's memory.

It wasn't until she was sitting beside him in the car on the way to Marjorie's house that she had the unwelcome thought that he had given the ear-rings and ring to her because his sister might have commented on her lack of jewellery. It was a sobering thought.

Marjorie lived in a rather splendid house in Richmond with her husband and four children. Araminta wondered if she was as nice as her sister and tried not to feel nervous. There was no need for that; she was welcomed warmly, kissed and embraced and laughed over, and swept upstairs to see the children: three boys and a girl. 'Twins, my dear,' explained Marjorie. 'The boys—

they're seven—then there's Piers, who is five, and our little Rosie—she's three.'

Marjorie was younger than Lydia but just as nice, thought Araminta, admiring all the children under the rather stern eye of an elderly nanny. She was whisked back downstairs then, and led into a room full of people.

'Old friends,' said Marjorie. 'They're all longing to meet Jason's wife!'

Jason took Araminta's arm and led her from one to the other of the guests, and his firm hand gave her confidence so that she lost her initial shyness and began to enjoy herself. She thought she was going to like everyone there, although she had her doubts about a pretty redhead, older than herself and strikingly dressed. 'This is Vicky,' Jason told her. 'We've known each other for a good many years now.'

Vicky kissed his cheek. 'Darling Jason, going behind my back like this and getting married—my heart's broken!' She smiled at Araminta. 'I do hope you'll be able to mend it, Araminta.'

Araminta smiled. 'I wouldn't have married him if I hadn't been sure of doing that!' she said lightly. She added mendaciously, 'Since you're an old friend of Jason's, I hope we'll be friends too.'

Vicky for once was uncertain. 'Oh, of course—we must have coffee some time. Or lunch. Jason used to take me to a delightful little restaurant—we might go there.'

Someone else joined them then, and presently she wandered off, leaving Jason faintly amused and Araminta at boiling-point. It rather suited her, for it gave her a pretty colour in her cheeks and added a decided sparkle to her dark eyes. When she was in a temper, he had noticed, they became almost black.

It was late by the time they got home, and Araminta wished Jason goodnight as they entered the hall.

'You enjoyed the evening?' he wanted to know.

'Yes, very much, thank you. I like Marjorie and your friends. I—I hope I did all the right things. I wouldn't like to let you down.'

He crossed the hall and took her hands in his. 'My dear Araminta, you were delightful—they all found you charming.'

It would be nice, reflected Araminta, if Jason found me charming too. Love, if this was love, wasn't at all what she had expected; any charms his friends might have seen in her were clearly not visible to him. She withdrew her hands gently, wished him goodnight once more and went upstairs.

Something would have to be done, and quickly, before that wretched Vicky got her elegant little claws into him. How, she wondered, did one get a man to fall in love with one—even show an interest...?

Something which the professor was doing, if only she could have known. There had been something about Araminta which had caused him to look at her thoughtfully during the evening. There had been something different about her; it was as though she had made a discovery of some sort. Whatever it was, she was keeping it to herself. He smiled a little; her goodnights had been friendly but brisk. That was what he liked about her, he decided, her lack of coyness, her matter-of-fact way of looking at things. He went to his study with the dogs and sat down to make some notes for his next lecture, dismissing her comfortably from his mind. All the same, as he went to his room later he reminded himself that they would go to the cottage the next weekend—

Araminta was good company and she had the gift of making herself invisible when he needed to work or read.

They left London the following Friday morning and, since they hoped to spend the weekend walking and pottering in the garden, Araminta wore the suede jacket and one of her new skirts with a silk shirt and cashmere sweater. She wore sensible shoes too, prudently added her Burberry and a headscarf, and added a plain jersey dress which the saleswoman had assured her would be most useful for countless occasions. One never knew, thought Araminta.

She hadn't seen much of Jason during the last day or so; he had been operating each day as well as seeing his private patients, and in the evenings she had sat quietly, saying little at their meal but listening while he talked.

'I don't bore you?' he had asked.

'No, I like to hear about your work. I don't always understand what you are saying but I can always look it up later on.'

He had laughed then. 'I really must arrange for you to come to the hospital.' He was kind and considerate to her. He had effortless good manners even when he was absorbed in his work, asking her how she had spent her day, suggesting things they might do together when he was free. Well, he's free now, she reflected as they drove through London, through its suburbs, and on to the Bishop's Stortford road.

The professor took the road to Saffron Walden from Bishops Stortford, and on reaching that small town turned into a narrow country road. He hadn't said much on their journey, but now he told her that they were only a mile or two from the village. 'It's rather charming,' he said. 'Ashdon lies in a valley with its church on a hill

above it. Our cottage is on the other side of the village—
ten minutes' walk away. It isn't isolated, but our nearest
neighbours are a couple of fields away. I hope you'll like
it.'

'I'm sure I shall.' Araminta found the countryside
charming. 'Do you come here for your holidays as well
as weekends?'

'The odd week, specially in the summer, but if you
would prefer it we can go abroad.'

'I've never been out of England,' said Araminta
cheerfully, 'and I don't know much of it. I shall be quite
happy going wherever you want to go.'

'I go away fairly frequently,' he observed. 'Seminars,
examining students—that kind of thing—and of course
consultations, and to operate.' He added, 'On my own,
of course.'

'Of course,' she agreed, and felt disquiet at the idea
of his being in some foreign country surrounded by
charming women. Would he have taken her with him,
she wondered, if he had loved her? Only time would tell
her that.

Ashdon was charming, with the Rose and Crown pub
overlooking a stream. The houses were old, its few shops
looked as though they had been there for a very long
time, and at the end of the village, halfway to the church,
Jason turned into a roughly surfaced lane, passed a house
or two and then, after a short distance, came to a halt
before a wide gate. He got out and opened it and drove
through to stop the car before the cottage door. It was
a solid door, rather narrow and low, with a porch and
seats on either side of it. The dogs were uttering happy
barks and he said, 'Don't get out for a moment and I'll
shut the gates—they always go a little mad when we
get here.'

Not surprising, thought Araminta; the cottage was charming. It was whitewashed and thatched, with a great many small windows, and, as far as she could see, the garden stretched on all sides. She was as impatient as the dogs to get out and look around, and she skipped out when Jason opened her door.

It was a splendid day and, although the wind was fresh and chilly, there were white clouds scudding across a blue sky. She took a deep breath and looked with pleasure at the flowerbeds crowded with daffodils, early tulips and great cushions of polyanthus.

'What a beautiful garden—Jason, it's lovely...'

He unlocked the cottage door. The dogs pushed and jostled to get in first, and she stood just inside the narrow hall and looked around her. There were doors on either side and another facing her which Jason opened, revealing a small kitchen. She peered over his shoulder and saw that it had a tiled floor, plastered walls and an old-fashioned white porcelain sink. There were red enamelled saucepans on a shelf and a small fridge beside a gas stove.

She nodded her neat head in approval. 'It wouldn't be right to modernise it too much.' She went past him to the door and opened it, anxious to see more of the garden.

There was a small, bedraggled cat on the step, almost skeletal in its thinness. It made no effort to run away but mewed soundlessly as she bent to pick it up. The dogs crowded round, and she tucked it securely in her arms and said urgently, 'Jason...'

He had been turning on the gas, but something in her voice made him go to her. 'Look,' said Araminta, 'she was on the doorstep—she's starving and I think she's going to have kittens. Oh, Jason...'

He took the little beast and laid it gently on the table.

'There should be milk in the fridge—can you warm a little?' He was examining the pathetic bundle with careful hands. When she brought the milk, he said, 'I don't think there's anything broken or damaged. She's certainly starved. Will you give her the milk, just a little at a time, while I find a box and papers? She's very cold. I'll light the fire in the sitting-room and we can keep an eye on her.'

'Goldie and Neptune?'

'They'll not harm her.' He went away and came back presently with a box lined with newspaper. The cat had taken the milk eagerly, and he lifted her into the box and left it on the table.

'She needs more food,' said Araminta. 'Shall I give her more milk?'

'Yes, and see if there's anything in the cupboard—tinned milk?—just a little.'

Araminta went to look; the cupboard was well-stocked. 'There's a tin of sago.'

'Splendid. Will you warm it while I bring in the bags and see to the dogs?'

Half an hour later, as they sat with the cat before the fire and the dogs on either side of the box and mugs of instant coffee in their hands, the professor observed, 'Rather a disrupted start to our weekend, I'm afraid.'

'I'm glad we came and I hope she'll be all right. How lucky you were here.' At his questioning look, she added, 'You knew what to do...'

He didn't answer her but said presently, 'I expect you would like to look round the cottage—Mrs Lott keeps it clean and the cupboard stocked.'

The sitting-room was small, with a couple of arm-chairs, a table or two, an alcove with its shelves lined with books, and a corner cupboard. There were several watercolours on its cream-painted walls, and the open fire. A cosy place, thought Araminta, getting up and following him from room to room. The other one held a round table with straight-backed rush-bottomed chairs, a sideboard and a smaller table under the lattice windows. Jason opened a door beside the fireplace and mounted the narrow twisting stairs, and Araminta, quite enchanted, skipped up behind him. There were two rooms leading off a tiny landing with a bathroom between. Both were simply furnished, but the curtains and coverlets were chintz and the rugs on the polished floors were pale and silky. Someone had furnished the little place with great care, and surely Jason wouldn't have known how to choose the pretty lampshades and the wall-sconces in every room? A woman's touch, thought Araminta, and I wonder whose. She asked guilelessly, 'I expect you have your friends to stay? It must be quite beautiful in the summer.'

The professor, who had put his spectacles on so that he might examine the books on one of the bedside tables, took them off to look at her. After a moment he said blandly, 'From time to time,' and watched her cheeks grow pink. She looked pretty, and for some reason he found that disturbing. 'I think you may prefer this room,' he added. 'There's a marvellous view. Shall we go down and see how our visitor is getting on?'

The cat was asleep; she looked pathetic but the professor pronounced her to be better. 'A week's good food and cosseting and she'll be splendid.'

'We can keep her?'

'Of course, isn't that what you want?'

'Yes, oh yes. Oh, Jason...' Araminta went bright red, mumbled about lunch and fled to the kitchen. She wasn't sure what she had been about to say, but whatever it was would have been disastrous; she would have to pull herself together. She began to poke around the cupboards and presently looked out of the window and saw him walking down the garden with a spade and the two dogs. She stared at his enormous back; wearing a sweater and wellies, he looked years younger. 'I must stop drooling,' Araminta told herself. 'If he wants a companion and a friend, he has me; if he'd wanted to fall in love he'd have chosen someone like Vicky.'

So over the entire weekend she maintained a determinedly friendly manner which, while it might have concealed her true feelings, caused an awkwardness which the professor was quick to notice and wonder about. He had to admit to himself that in the short time in which he had known her she had become a part of his life which was becoming increasingly important to him, but he was aware that she was keeping him at arm's length. They were still on excellent terms; they tended the cat together, dug the garden, went walking with the dogs and went to church on Sunday morning, but Araminta had retreated and he couldn't think why.

As they drove back on Sunday evening, the dogs on either side of the cat's basket on the back seat, he asked casually, 'You enjoyed our weekend? You are quite happy, Araminta?'

She said rather too quickly, 'Oh, yes, I'm very happy, Jason. It was a lovely weekend and your cottage is beautiful...'

'Our cottage,' he corrected her. 'If you would like to look round the hospital, I've an outpatients' clinic in the afternoon on Tuesday; you could spend an hour or so there and pick me up at the end of the clinic.'

'I'd like that very much. I won't be in the way?'

'No, no. Theatre's closed on Tuesday afternoons. I'll speak to Sister.' Another step in the right direction, thought Araminta—to know something of his day at the hospital. Perhaps Theatre Sister would give her a few clues...

Buller welcomed them back with dignity, received the information that a cat had been added to the household, and took the dogs away for their meal, the cat in her basket in his hand. He assured them that Mrs Buller would feed the little beast and wait for the professor's wishes as to its future.

'Mrs Buller won't mind?' asked Araminta anxiously.

'Not in the least. Come down and we'll have a drink before dinner.'

There were messages for him on the side-table in the hall; usually he took them straight to the study, but now he went into the drawing-room and sat down in his chair, holding them unopened in his hand. The weekend had been delightful; he had gone frequently to the cottage on his own, but with Araminta for company he had felt contented and relaxed. She had been happy, cooking their meals and making beds, helping in the garden, caring for the cat. All the same, there was something... She had looked charming at the cottage, wrapped in a pinny, bending over the stove; washing dishes was something he was quite unaccustomed to, but he had enjoyed the chore with her, drying the plates while they planned their day. He frowned. She had fitted into his life like a hand in a glove.

He took his spectacles from a pocket and began to read the first of the messages. He was interrupted by a slightly flustered Buller, swept aside by Vicky as she came into the room.

'Darling Jason, say you're glad to see me. I've had the dullest weekend and I'm bored to death, so I've come to share your dinner.' She glanced around her. 'Where's Araminta? She won't mind, will she?'

The professor put down his notes with a sigh. 'We are just back from the cottage,' he said as he got up. 'I'm sure Araminta will be delighted to invite you to dinner—she will be down in a minute.'

Vicky pouted. 'You don't sound very pleased to see me. Have you turned into a dreary old married man already?'

He smiled thinly. 'Here is Araminta.'

Araminta had changed into one of her pretty dresses and put on a pair of high-heeled shoes, something she was glad of when she saw Vicky. Her greeting wasn't to be faulted, and when Jason said that Vicky would like to stay for dinner, she said at once, 'Oh, how nice, of course she must. I'll tell Mrs Buller.' She smiled widely at them both and took herself off to the kitchen to discuss with Mrs Buller how dinner cooked for two could be stretched to three. When she went back to the drawing-room, Vicky was sitting close to Jason, chattering in her high voice and laughing a great deal.

He got up as Araminta joined them. 'Time for a drink before we eat—what will you have, Vicky?'

'Have you forgotten already? Gin and tonic, of course—unless there's champagne.'

He handed her the drink and turned to Araminta. 'Sherry for you, my dear?'

'Please, Jason.' She sat quietly, not attempting to compete with Vicky's light-hearted gossip, for the most part about people she had never heard of, mutual ac-quaintances of Jason and Vicky.

It was brought to an end by Jason's quiet, 'What a chatterbox you are, Vicky.' He glanced across at Araminta. 'Is our little cat quite comfortable?'

'Yes, she's asleep by the Aga.' Araminta turned to Vicky. 'We found a cat at the cottage—the poor thing was half starved and going to have kittens—we brought her back here to live with us.'

Vicky wrinkled her pretty nose. 'Darling, are you one of those dreadful do-gooders who go around rescuing animals and giving money to beggars? How absolutely dire.' She turned a laughing face to the professor. 'Jason, did you know Araminta was so—so worthy when you married her?'

The professor's mouth was a thin line but he spoke quite quietly. 'What a peculiar remark to make, Vicky, and I'm afraid you must consider me worthy too, for I also rescue animals and give money to beggars—Araminta and I are completely in accord over that.'

He had spoken without seeming to look at Araminta, who had gone an unhappy pink; now he smiled across at her. 'Isn't that so, darling?'

The 'darling' was a surprise and took her breath, but she nodded and smiled. He didn't mean it, of course, he was saying it to squash Vicky's spite. She lifted her chin and said to Vicky, 'I expect you have any number of friends?'

'Hundreds.' She sounded sulky. 'I scarcely have a moment to myself. Life's too short not to get as much fun out of it as possible.'

There was no need to answer that, for Buller came to say that dinner was served, and they went into the dining-room and ate the garlic mushrooms, rack of lamb and peach pavlova. The professor kept the talk general, which gave their guest no chance to get personal.

Over coffee Vicky said, 'You'll drive me home, won't you, Jason? I had a taxi here—there's never anywhere to park a car...'

'It will have to be a taxi back,' he told her. 'I'm on call and must stay at home, I'm afraid. Buller shall get you a taxi.'

She was in no hurry to leave, however, and when the door finally closed behind her Jason collected up his notes. 'I'll have to see to these,' he told Araminta, 'if you'll forgive me. A wasted evening...'

Araminta wasn't sure if he meant that Vicky had wasted his evening or if he had intended to spend it in his study. She murmured a nothing and said that she would go to bed. Her goodnight was cheerful, and she added, 'It was a lovely weekend—thank you for taking me, Jason.'

He came to the foot of the stairs. 'Thank me?' He sounded harsh. 'Why should you thank me? I found every moment of it delightful.'

He turned away and closed the study door after him and she went on upstairs, thinking over his words. It was early days, but was he at least noticing her? Although I can quite see why he married me, she reflected, to escape from women like Vicky; I'm a buffer, aren't I? The thing is to make the buffer attractive.

She laid her head on her pillow and slept at once, sure that she had at least one foot in the door, as it were.

The professor came home at lunchtime on Tuesday and drove Araminta to the hospital, where he handed her over to Theatre Sister, a tall, stout lady with iron-grey hair, small, twinkling blue eyes and an extremely brisk manner.

'Take care of her,' he said to Sister Weekes. 'I'll be finished around five o'clock if you'll send her down to OPD.'

He went away and Araminta started on her tour. Sister Weekes was a good guide and she was willing to answer Araminta's questions. In reply to the query as to how long she had worked with Jason she laughed. 'Years, my dear. I can remember him when he was a houseman here; always had his nose in a book, very studious, although he played rugger for the hospital. There was no holding him back, of course—got the best brain I've ever come across and knows how to use it. Glad he's married; the girls have been after him for ten years and, since he spends his leisure with his nose in a book, he might easily have found himself married to one of them without realising it. He'll be happy with you, though.'

Araminta said faintly, 'I do hope so,' and then, more strongly, 'But he did know he was marrying me, if you see what I mean.'

'Never did a better thing in his life,' declared her companion. 'Shall we go to the children's wards?'

By the time they reached OPD the vast hall was almost empty. 'Still at it?' asked Sister Weekes. 'Sit down here, my dear, he won't be long now. I'll have to go, I'm afraid. A pleasure meeting you—come again whenever you want to. I'll probably be in Theatre, but there's no reason why you shouldn't poke around on your own.'

She sailed away and Araminta sat on one of the benches and watched as the last handful of patients went one by one through the doors at the end of the hall. Presently Jason came out, looking quite different in a long white coat with a stethoscope hanging round his neck. He had a sister with him and an arm full of folders, and when he saw her he called, 'I'll be with you in a moment, Araminta,' and disappeared through another door.

'You haven't been waiting long?' he asked as he returned presently and, when she said no, asked if she had enjoyed herself.

'Yes, oh, yes. I had no idea. I wish I were a nurse so that I could work with you.' She had spoken without thinking, and blushed at the silliness of her remark.

'So do I,' said Jason softly. 'On the other hand, I'd rather have you to come home to, Araminta.'

He was staring at her so intently that she looked down at her person. 'Is something wrong?' she asked him.

'No, no, something is very right and I've only just discovered it.'

'Oh, good. I expect you are pleased when things go right. Do you want to go home now?' She stood up, admired her shoes for a moment, and then looked up at him. 'I like your Sister Weekes.'

'So do I. She's a martinet in Theatre but she has a heart of gold.'

Back at the house, Araminta went off to see how the cat was faring.

'Two kittens,' Mrs Buller told her. 'Little dears, and she's fine, ma'am. But she needs a bit of feeding up.'

'The professor will be pleased.' She hurried to tell him and he went back to the kitchen with her, bending over the box, his arm round Araminta's shoulder.

'She'll do. Do you feel like a quick walk when we've had tea?'

The rest of the evening they spent together, and Araminta went to bed almost happy. Jason didn't just like her, he was actually enjoying being with her. She lay awake for a while, deciding what she should wear the next day—it was very important to make herself as attractive as possible. She couldn't compete with someone like Vicky, but bread and butter made a nice change from cream cakes, and she didn't think Jason was partial to too many cakes...

CHAPTER NINE

ARAMINTA got up early so that she had plenty of time to arrange her hair just so, do her face carefully and get into a knitted two-piece in a pleasing shade of brown. It had been very expensive but worth every penny, she decided, surveying her person before going down to breakfast.

Indeed Jason gave her a second and lingering glance as she sat down. He wondered why he hadn't seen that she was really rather pretty. Also so restful, he concluded, as he opened his letters.

Araminta had seen the second look and felt satisfaction. Given a month or so and no interference from Vicky, another weekend at the cottage, and regular visits to the hairdresser, there might be real progress. She had no great opinion of her powers to attract, but love had given her a strong determination. She ate her breakfast, leaving him to read his post in peace.

She was in the kitchen just before teatime, feeding the cat, when Buller came to find her. 'Miss Alice Smith has called, ma'am. I've put her in the drawing-room.'

'My sister? Oh, thank you, Buller. Could we have tea presently, please?'

Alice was fingering the small silver ornaments set out on a small ebony side-table. She turned round as Araminta went in. 'Landed on your feet, haven't you?'

'Hello,' said Araminta. 'It's nice to see you, Alice. You'll stay for tea?'

'That's why I came—well, partly. I wanted to see where you were living before we go.'

'Go where?'

'Father's being transferred to Bournemouth—promotion. More money too.'

'He's pleased?'

'You bet he is. What's more, he's had an offer for the house. You're not the only one to live on easy street.' Alice abandoned her restless wandering and sat down near the fire. She gave a little laugh. 'Been shopping too...'

'Yes. Will you like living in Bournemouth, Alice?'

'Rather. Plenty going on there. I might even get some sort of job—a boutique or something like that.'

'When is Father going? Is he coming to say goodbye?'

Alice shrugged. 'I don't know—he's fed up with you leaving us in the lurch.'

It was a good thing that Buller brought in the tea then, for Araminta was on the point of answering that. She stayed silent and poured their tea and handed scones and tiny sandwiches and a rich chocolate cake, while Alice talked of the new clothes she was going to buy.

'You'll miss your friends,' said Araminta.

'No, I shan't. I'll soon have new friends and plenty of men to take me out. They like a pretty face. I could have got your old professor if I'd wanted him.'

'Presumably you didn't want him!' said Jason from the doorway. 'Welcome to our home, Alice.' He crossed the room and bent to kiss Araminta. 'I'm home early,' he told her, 'and I hope it won't upset your arrangements if an old friend of mine and his wife come to dinner?'

Buller came in with fresh tea and Jason sat down with the dogs beside him. It was Araminta who spoke. 'Alice came to tell me that Father has got promotion—they're going to live in Bournemouth.'

'Indeed? Will you like that, Alice?'

'Yes, and so will Father. We're going quite soon, as soon as the house is sold.'

'Perhaps a little difficult in these times?' he suggested blandly.

'We've got a buyer.'

'Splendid. Perhaps before you go you will be our guests for dinner?'

'At a restaurant? Will you phone Father and fix a date? It'll have to be soon.'

'Tomorrow evening? I'll book a table in the hope that it suits him. Would you ask him to give me a ring this evening?'

'Where are we going?'

'What about the Gay Hussar?' He turned to Araminta. 'You'd like that, my dear?'

'It sounds delightful.'

Alice got to her feet. 'I bought a new dress the other day, and now I can wear it. It's a dressy sort of place, isn't it? I must get my bus.'

'Short and pretty, I should think,' said Araminta.

'Buller will get you a taxi,' said the professor, and submitted to Alice's kiss.

She didn't kiss Araminta but waved her fingers at her with a 'See you tomorrow evening, thanks for the tea.'

Araminta stood at the door with Jason and watched the taxi drive away. In the hall she said, 'That was very kind of you to invite Father and Alice to dinner. I—I was a bit surprised to see her but it's such good news that Father has promotion. I think they'll be very happy at Bournemouth and he's sold the house—it seems like a miracle.'

She glanced at him and found him looking at her with a half-smile.

'It wasn't a miracle,' she said slowly. 'You've done it all, haven't you? You said "Leave it to me" and I did, but I never thought... Why did you go to so much trouble?'

'I wanted to make you happy, Araminta.' He was standing very close to her, looking down on to her enquiring face.

'You have, oh, you have, Jason. Thank you very much indeed. I can't thank you enough. Was it very difficult?'

'No, no. I do know a number of people and they know other people, so sooner or later one gets in touch with the right person.'

'Father doesn't know it was you...?'

'Certainly not, nor must he be told. You agree?'

'Yes, of course I do. Is the Gay Hussar the kind of place where you dress up?'

'A pretty dress will do.'

'I wouldn't want to outshine Alice—well, I can't do that, she's so pretty, but you know what I mean.'

'I'm sure you will wear exactly the right frock,' he assured her solemnly.

Her choice, it seemed, was just right—silk jersey, very plainly cut; its colour was stone, the height of fashion and, mindful of Alice's feelings, she didn't wear the diamond ear-rings, only her ring. She and Jason made an elegant pair as they went into the restaurant and were shown to their table. Jason had arranged for a taxi to bring Alice and her father, and barely a minute later they arrived. Her father looked very much at his ease; he was a good-looking man and well-dressed, and Alice walked beside him, aware that she was gathering admiring looks, smiling radiantly, knowing that her pale blue dress became her. The professor stood up to welcome them and Araminta's father stooped to kiss her cheek. There was no warmth in his greeting but he shook hands with Jason, fussed over Alice and then looked around him. It was obvious that he had no intention of saying much to Araminta, and after a brief silence the professor took affairs into his own hands, ordering drinks, making conversation, drawing Araminta into it with effortless ease.

Once the meal was started it became easier, and when Alice had had a glass of wine after her sherry, she started to talk about her plans for Bournemouth. She was full of ideas and certain that life there would be exactly as she planned and presently her father joined in. The professor, listening gravely to what they had to say, knowing most of it already, encouraged them to talk so that, after those first few awkward moments, the dinner party was a success.

Only as they stood in the foyer, waiting for the taxi and saying goodbye, did Mr Smith say suddenly to Araminta, 'Of course, you treated us very badly, my dear. I am surprised that any daughter of mine could be so cold-hearted and ungenerous, leaving us to manage on our own. However, I shall say no more about it; Alice and I will do very well at Bournemouth, but I find it hard to forget your selfishness even if I can forgive.'

Araminta was thankful that Jason and Alice were standing a little apart and hadn't heard this. She said quietly, 'Goodbye, Father. I'm glad you have such a promising future,' and saw with relief that the taxi had arrived.

It wasn't until they were driving back home that Jason asked, 'What did your father say to upset you, Araminta?'

'Oh, nothing much, I'm sure he didn't mean it.' She turned her head away, fighting a wish to weep. 'They did enjoy themselves. Thank you for inviting them, Jason.'

He said harshly, 'Unless you wish to do so, you do not have to see your father or Alice again. They have treated you badly, used you as a housekeeper and bread-winner, and shown not one jot of gratitude. They do not deserve to have their circumstances improved but it was the only way I could think of that would set you free.'

He had set her free when he married her but she didn't say so and, before she could even speak, he went on in his usual calm way. 'Would you like to come to my rooms tomorrow afternoon? I've several patients to see but I should be through by four o'clock. I'd like you to meet Mrs Wells and Mrs Dunn—they have been with me for years and they're dying of curiosity about you.'

'I'd like that. Are your rooms close by? Can I walk there?'

'Easily, but I'll be home for lunch. I'll drive you there and we can come home together.'

'Oh, good. I won't be in the way?'

'No, Araminta.' The certainty in his voice left her content.

When she went down to breakfast the next morning it was to find him already gone. 'Needed at the hospital,' Buller told her. 'Left the house soon after I was up, ma'am. I was to tell you that he'll be home for lunch but to make it one o'clock.'

There was plenty to keep her busy during the morning: the dogs to walk, flowers to arrange, Mrs Buller to see, the cat and kittens to attend to. All the same, the hours dragged before she would see Jason again.

'Just remember why he married you, my girl,' she reminded her reflection as she tidied her hair and checked her make-up. 'Companionship, friendship, and someone to talk to...'

He was a little late for lunch, but nothing in his manner betrayed that he had been operating since before eight o'clock that morning. 'A nasty road accident,' he told her. 'Teenagers in a stolen car.'

'Tell me about it.'

Since she obviously wanted to know, he told her and, when he had finished, he said, 'What a good listener you are, Araminta,' and smiled as he added, 'But that is partly why I married you, isn't it?'

He spoke casually but he watched her from under his lids as he spoke.

'That's right. But you see, I am really interested—I want to know about your work.' That sounded a bit too enthusiastic. 'I think perhaps I would have liked to have trained as a nurse.'

Jason's rooms were in Wigmore Street, in a tall red-brick house with a dignified entrance and well-polished brass plates beside the door. He led her up a flight of stairs and opened a door on the landing. The waiting-room, comfortably furnished with flowers here and there, was light and airy, the windows curtained in a pretty flowery chintz. Reassuring, thought Araminta, and soothing to a nervous patient. Mrs Wells was there, and so was Mrs Dunn, both cosily shaped, with kind faces and severe hair-styles. It wasn't until Araminta was shaking hands with them that she acknowledged the fear that they might have been willowy young women with beautiful legs and lovely faces.

They carried her off to a small room behind the waiting-room and sat her down. 'You'll have a cup of tea, Mrs Lister? We are so very glad to meet you. I must just pop back and see if the professor wants anything and show in the first patient, then I'll be back and Dolly will have to go into the consulting-room.' Mrs Wells beamed at Araminta. 'We have been so anxious for the dear professor to marry—a family man at heart despite his books, we have always said, and that lovely house, just right for little children.'

There was more than enough room for half a dozen, thought Araminta, three of each, and the little girls would be blue-eyed and fair-haired and beautiful...

'Such a joy, I always think,' Mrs Wells was saying, 'and in such a pretty village.' She was looking rather anxiously at Araminta, who made haste to agree although she wasn't sure what she was agreeing about.

Mrs Dunn nodded her head in a pleased way as Mrs Wells went away, to return presently so that Mrs Dunn could take her place. 'We'll have a cup of tea now, shall we? Dolly will be some time with the patient—she's rather elderly.' She poured the tea. 'How do you like being a doctor's wife? Well, I should say surgeon, shouldn't I? And a busy one too—such a shame that you don't see more of each other. My hubby was a chemist so he had regular hours.' Just for a moment she looked wistful. 'There's nothing like a happy marriage. Me and Dolly, we've been lucky and still are, for the professor is so considerate. There's nothing we wouldn't do for him.'

Araminta accepted more tea. She had wanted to know as much as possible about Jason; here were rich pickings.

She asked, 'Have you both been working for him for a long time?'

Mrs Wells was only too glad to gossip and, when she was at her desk, Mrs Dunn was in and out. Araminta learned a good deal about Jason, things that she thought he might not tell her himself: hours on end at a railway crash, lying under the wreckage of a huge transporter, amputating a leg so that the driver might be freed, being lowered from a helicopter on to a giant wheel at a funfair to deal with a child's head injuries. There were countless incidents about which he had never spoken except, of necessity, to his two faithful helpers.

Later, when the last patient had gone, he came to fetch her, and she had such a strong urge to fling her arms round his neck and tell him how much she loved him that she could only nod and smile when he asked her if she had enjoyed meeting Mrs Wells and Mrs Dunn.

A week went by, during which Araminta had ample time to realise that concealing her true feelings from Jason while at the same time doing her best to make him fall in love with her was going to be fraught with hazardous moments. Once or twice she had caught him looking at her in a thoughtful manner, rather like a doctor not quite sure of his diagnosis, but not, to her regret, in the least lover-like. On the other hand, he had taken to sitting with her after dinner in the evenings, immersed in a book, it was true. She took pains with her appearance, taking care to sit so that the gentle rose-coloured light from the lamp on her table shone on to whichever of the new dresses she was wearing. Not that he would notice, she reflected.

The professor did notice. Immersed in the newspapers or the poems of Juvenal—in the original of course—he yet found the opportunity to watch Araminta sitting there, the picture of tranquillity, stitching away at her tapestry. It was a pity she never looked up, for then she would have seen that his manner wasn't in the least thoughtful, so they sat, the pair of them, each concealing their true feelings, entirely at cross-purposes.

All the same, they were the best of friends, exchanging their day's news each evening, and Araminta, primed by the books he had found for her, was beginning to understand what he was talking about while he listened with inward amusement to her accounts of coffee-mornings and afternoon teas with his colleagues' wives. They were kind to her, she told him, although some of the older wives were a little overpowering.

'We'll give a dinner party,' he told her, 'but not just yet. I thought we might go to the cottage again...'

'I'd like that—when?'

'This weekend, if that suits you? I'll be free on Saturday and Sunday.'

The weather began to worsen towards the weekend but they decided to go just the same. They left on Friday evening in pouring rain and a fierce wind, which seemed fiercer once they had left the city behind them and were driving through the flat Essex countryside. They reached the cottage without mishap to find that Mrs Lott had left a meal ready to be warmed up, the fire laid and the central heating on. They had brought the dogs with them, but Blossom the cat and her kittens had been left in Mrs Buller's care. Araminta went from room to room turning the lights on, while Jason lit the fire and then took the dogs for a run while she got the supper. The three of them came back presently, wringing wet.

'It's turning nasty,' observed Jason. 'Let's see what the weather forecast is.'

'A rapid deterioration in the weather,' said a serious forecaster. 'Storm-force winds likely to sweep across the country within the next twenty-four hours.' There would probably be damage to buildings; people were advised to secure their homes and avoid travelling unless it was necessary.

'We had better go home tomorrow morning,' said Jason as they sat at supper. 'I'm going to make everything secure here and we can leave as soon as possible.' He spoke easily. 'I think it best if we return early. I've a list on Monday morning.'

Araminta hid disappointment. She had been looking forward to a day or two with him away from phone calls and emergencies, to say nothing of the hours he spent in his study. He would have time to talk to her. What about, she had no idea, but if there was nothing else to attract his attention he might take rather more interest in her as a person. 'That seems sensible,' she observed. 'I've not unpacked the bags yet. What a good thing.'

After their meal the professor went out again with the remark that he would be back presently, but it was half an hour before he returned, very wet.

'Where have you been? You're wringing wet again.' Araminta sounded so like a nagging wife that he smiled. 'I've battened down the garden shed and the coal-shed, and moved everything which can be moved into the lean-to. I went down to the village and saw Mrs Lott, and told her that I would shut off everything before we go so that she won't need to come here until the weather improves.'

'The cottage will be all right? The roof...?'

'Thatch, my dear. Pretty safe, and the walls are thick. The weather's worsening, though. Suppose we leave after breakfast—nine o'clock suit you?'

She bade him goodnight and went upstairs to her bed, leaving everything ready for their breakfast in the morning. She would get up early and empty the fridge and pack away the tins and packets—things which would come to no harm if they were stored for some time. The wind was howling round the cottage as she got into bed, and she had expected that it would keep her awake, but she was asleep within five minutes, her last thoughts of Jason, as they always were.

A hand on her shoulder brought her upright in the dark room, lighted by the torch the professor held. 'My dear, I'm sorry to wake you. We have to go back as soon as possible. Lydia phoned—how the lines are still working is a miracle—Jimmy is missing. The river has broken its banks and parts of Tisbury are under water. He's been staying with a friend on the other side and the friend's parents phoned her to say that their boy came back a few hours ago and Jimmy wasn't with him. Lydia is distraught. I must go and see what I can do...'

Araminta tossed her hair over her shoulder. 'Of course you must. What's the time?'

'Five o'clock. I'll make tea while you dress.' He went away and she shot out of bed and into her clothes, tied back her hair with a handy piece of string and hurried downstairs. Jason was in the kitchen, pouring hot water into the teapot. 'Thank heaven we've got gas.' He put their mugs on the table and put down water for the dogs. 'Can you be ready in ten minutes?'

'Yes.' She opened the fridge door and began to load its contents into the box they had brought with them. She was as good as her word. She was ready, her Burberry closely belted, a scarf tied over her head and the dogs beside her when he came in, closing the door against the gale.

He loaded their bags and the box and came back for the dogs, clipping on their leads. 'In case we need to get out of the car,' he explained in his unhurried way. 'Stay there and I'll come for you.'

It was dark in the cottage for there was no electricity. It seemed like hours instead of minutes before Jason came back with the torch, and Araminta had her teeth clenched on a scream, but his unworried, 'Ready? Don't let go of me once we're outside or you'll be blown over,' reassured her.

She had no intention of letting go; she clung like a limpet as they went outside. The car was very close; he opened the door and tossed her in as though she had been a feather, made his way round the bonnet and got in beside her, fastened her seatbelt and switched on.

'Did you turn off the gas and electricity?' asked Araminta and he laughed.

'What's so funny?' she asked edgily.

'No, no, not funny, I find it so reassuring that you should think of it—as though we were going on holiday and you were having last-minute doubts about leaving the family home. I am delighted to see that you are not prone to hysterics when things go a little wrong.'

'I was about to scream when you came back,' said Araminta, ever truthful.

The professor turned to look at her. The scarf tied tightly over unbrushed hair did nothing to enhance her ordinary face, pale with fright. He thought that she looked beautiful. He sent the big car forward carefully, but not before he had bent to kiss her.

She sat like a mouse, not moving a muscle as he drove through the lane, already flooded in places, and when the headlights revealed a fallen tree only yards ahead she made no sign as he reversed back up the narrow road until he reached a crossroads. 'Look at the map,' he told her. 'The signpost says Little Mitchford—can we work round through there back to the Bishop's Stortford road?'

'Yes.' She was peering at the map with the aid of a torch. 'At Little Mitchford you'll have to turn left to Great Winley...'

'If I can. We'll have a go!'

It was lighter now, as light as it would get for some time, the sky leaden and menacing, and Jason switched on the radio.

'Severe storms,' said a cheerful voice, 'increasing in the west of the country, causing severe flooding; minor roads blocked by fallen trees; drivers are urged to stay at home unless their journey is absolutely necessary.'

'Could we go by train?' began Araminta.

The voice continued, 'Train services to the south and west of the country are seriously disrupted.'

'I'll take the car, Araminta,' said the professor, and added, 'I shall go alone.'

Araminta, who had no intention of allowing him to do any such thing, said, 'Yes, Jason,' and then, 'We turn off here to Great Winley.'

They finally gained the main road, almost empty of traffic, but they were driving into the wind now and it slowed their progress; nonetheless Jason drew up before their front door soon after eight o'clock.

'A hot bath for you, Araminta and a few hours in bed. But we'll have breakfast first, shall we?'

'I'll tell Buller. You're going to Tisbury?'

'Of course, but breakfast first.'

A worried Buller came into the hall as they went in with the dogs. He said, 'Good morning, ma'am, professor. We were a little worried. You'll be needing a good breakfast. Very nasty weather outside.'

'Very nasty,' agreed his master. He looked at Araminta. 'Breakfast in twenty minutes, my dear?'

Araminta, the picture of wifely acqiescence, said yes, and watched him throw off his wet raincoat and go into the drawing-room to let the dogs out into the garden. Upstairs she tore out of her clothes, showered in less than no time and dressed again, this time in tartan trousers and a thick pullover. Buller had taken their Burberrys to dry, and her wellies were still in the car. She unpacked her shoulder-bag and packed it again with spare undies, toothbrush, comb and a torch, bundled her hair into a plait and found a thick woollen scarf and gloves. With five minutes to spare she was downstairs again, leaving the bag, scarf and gloves in her room.

Jason had changed too. He glanced up as she joined him in the drawing-room and they went to have breakfast. 'You need not have dressed again—a dressing-gown would have done well enough. In fact, you could have had breakfast in bed—I should have thought of that.'

'It's nice to feel warm again,' said Araminta chattily, 'and I'm famished.' She applied herself to breakfast and made no effort to talk. Jason was looking thoughtful, probably deciding the best way to get to Tisbury.

They didn't linger over their meal. As they left the dining-room he said, 'I'll be off now. Don't worry if you don't hear anything, probably the phone won't be working, but I'll keep in touch as soon as I can from the car.'

He had stopped to fondle the dogs, and started to get into his Burberry.

Araminta said nothing but skipped upstairs, to appear in no time at all clad for the journey.

His frown might have intimidated anyone less determined than Araminta. 'I'm coming with you,' she told him.

'Indeed you are not...' His voice was icy.

'You'll need someone to hold the torch and open the car doors—and go for help. I'm coming. I'm sorry if it annoys you. I won't say a word in the car and I'm not a bit frightened when you're driving.'

'You have no need to butter me up.' He sounded outraged.

'Don't be silly,' said Araminta. 'I'm sensible and strong and another pair of hands, which I'm sure you will need when we get there. I'm coming.'

'I don't want you with me, Araminta.'

'I know that, but you'll just have to put up with me!'

'It will probably be dangerous.'

She gave him a long look. 'That's why I'm coming,' she told him quietly. 'We're wasting time...'

He wrapped her round with his great arms. 'If anything should happen...' he said half-angrily, but she didn't care; it was like being held close by a very solid tree. In a Burberry, she reflected absurdly.

'Nothing will happen,' she muttered into his shoulder.

He ran a gentle finger down her cheek. 'Let's go,' he said.

It wasn't until they were clear of London and its suburbs that the full force of the storm made itself felt. The rain beat relentlessly against the windscreen and they could see the flooded fields on either side of the motorway. There were trees lying uprooted, and several times Jason had to brake to avoid falling branches, but the car held the road well and, since Jason appeared unperturbed, Araminta did her best to imitate him. They didn't talk; it was hardly a situation where conversation was required, and they had said all that there was to say for the moment.

After what seemed to her to be a lifetime, they reached the Tisbury turn-off and found the road for the most part under water. It was strewn with debris from the storm as well, and twice Jason stopped the car to get out and haul aside branches lying across the road. It was noon by now and there were no signs of the storm's dying down; it was still raining as hard as ever and the sky hung like a dark grey blanket over their heads. Araminta, peering from her window, just hoped that Jason knew the way, for there were narrow roads every mile or so and lanes running off in all directions, all awash. It was with relief that she glimpsed a glimmer of light and saw that they were passing scattered houses, most of them with candles in their windows. 'Tisbury,' said Jason, and looked at the car clock. 'Almost one o'clock.'

Araminta, practical and hungry, observed that it was lunchtime, and he laughed. 'You have hidden depths which continue to astonish me, my dear.' He drove slowly now as they neared the village, and she sat wondering just what he had meant. Obviously he wasn't going to tell her then. The road was fairly clear of water but, as they reached the top of the hill leading down to the shops and station, she could see that the flood-water was deep there. He turned the car up the hill and presently stopped before Lydia's door.

Lydia flung the door open as he got out and went to open Araminta's door. 'Jason, oh, Jason. The phone's out of order and Jimmy's gone—I know he is.' She burst into tears. 'I don't know what to do...'

'Stop crying, Lydia, and tell us just what has happened, then we can go and look for Jimmy.'

They had all gone into the kitchen, where the table was littered with plates and mugs and something was boiling dry on the gas stove. Araminta turned it off. 'Shall I make us all a cup of tea while you tell Jason what happened?'

Lydia sat down at the table. 'I haven't been able to do anything—I'd love a cup of tea. Dear Araminta, so sensible...'

Jason had taken off his Burberry and helped Araminta with hers. 'A quick meal?' he suggested softly. 'We can eat and talk at the same time—we can't rush off until we have some idea of where to go.'

Araminta put eggs on to boil, made toast, cleared the dishes off the table and washed the mugs. 'Where is Gloria?' she asked.

'Thank heaven, she's staying with friends in Bath. Jimmy was spending the weekend with the Dempsters— you know—on the other side of the river.' Lydia mopped her eyes and blew her nose. 'He and Philip Dempster went off for a hike after school yesterday afternoon, although the Dempsters tried to stop them, but you know what boys are... Philip didn't get back until late in the evening. He said Jimmy had fallen and hurt his leg— somewhere—oh, miles away and no roads—you know where I mean: woods and rough fields and the river running through the middle.' She paused and gulped and Araminta put a mug of tea in her hand, passed one to Jason, and dished up the eggs.

'I couldn't eat,' said Lydia, weeping again.

'I dare say there'll be a lot for you to do when we bring Jimmy back,' said Araminta in a sensible voice. 'You will feel more like getting his room ready and planning a meal if you've eaten something yourself.'

Lydia smiled at her. 'I think you must be Jason's treasure,' she said, and took a piece of toast.

'We'll need to cross the river,' said Jason.

'The bridge is down; the Dempsters phoned just before the line went dead. They said it may have caved in and they didn't dare to take the car across.'

'Had Philip any idea how far away they were when Jimmy hurt himself?'

'He thought about two miles, but he was ages getting back—he had to go round the worst of the floods.'

'I'll take the car as far as the bridge and take a look...' He caught Araminta's eye and smiled a little. 'All right, we'll take a look. The sooner the better.'

They had to drive down into the village before they could turn off towards the bridge, and the river and the floods were deep here. Araminta curled her toes in her wellies in speechless terror as they reached the bridge and Jason stopped the car in the swirling water. 'I'll cast an eye on the damage before we go over,' he told her cheerfully, and got out of the car.

It was a narrow bridge built of stone, and the flood-water was fast enveloping it. She watched Jason go to the end and then turn and come slowly back. He got into the car again. 'I think we might risk it. There's that piece of higher ground on the other side; we can park there and walk.'

Araminta closed her eyes as they went over the bridge, her teeth clenched so tightly that her jaws ached. 'You can look now,' said Jason, and parked the car on a rough bit of ground away from the worst of the flood.

It was like a nightmare. If it hadn't been for Jason's large hand holding hers firmly she would have turned and run. The wind seemed to strike at her from all sides and she couldn't see for the blinding rain. At least she could cry without its being noticed, the tears streaming down her cheeks to mingle with the rain. Presently she began to feel better. Jason seemed to know where he was going, forging ahead in the teeth of the wind, taking her with him. She supposed that there was a path, but since there was water all over the place it wasn't visible. There was no point in asking where they were going either; she would never be able to make herself heard above the wind. She squelched along, her feet sopping inside the wellies because the water had splashed over them, and she discovered that she was really rather happy.

What would happen, she wondered, if she were to stand still and tell Jason that she loved him? Only of course it wasn't possible; the wind would sweep her off her feet and, even if it quietened down long enough for her to tell him, she would still have to shout—one should declare one's love in a shy whisper, preferably in a pretty dress, with soft lighting. A tug on her arm brought her back to the realities of life. Jason was changing course, going towards a copse beside the river, which was bedraggled and a foot deep in muddy water.

They hadn't struggled halfway through when Araminta gave a small shriek. 'There he is—look. Wedged between that fallen tree and those bushes.'

He was conscious too, cold and wet and in pain, but alive. One leg was doubled up under him, though, and the professor squatted down beside him to take a look. First he took a flask from his pocket and poured some of its contents down Jimmy's throat before handing it to Araminta. She took a mouthful and caught her breath and gave him a reproachful look, which he ignored, before he took a pull himself. 'Now to work,' he said cheerfully. 'Jimmy, we will have to hurt you before we can get you out of here...'

'Shall I go back and get a stretcher and some people?' suggested Araminta.

Jason glanced at the swollen river racing past, carrying trees and wooden boxes, a hen-coop, and a mass of debris besides, and then he looked at her. She gulped— of course, the river was rising all the time, and before help could reach them, even if she could get back on her own, the flood would be upon them. She said, 'What do you want me to do?' and glowed at his smile.

He told her. Jimmy fainted when Jason took out a knife and cut off his shoe, which was fortunate for him, and Araminta, holding his leg steady while Jason straightened it until she heard the bones grate together, felt queasy. 'Don't leave go,' she was warned, as he took a plastic pack from somewhere under his Burberry, eased it on to the leg and inflated it, strapped it firmly, and stood up. He helped her to her numbed feet and just for a moment held her close. He kissed the tip of her nose. 'You will have to hang on to my coattails,' he shouted above the storm, and bent to heave the still-unconscious Jimmy on to his shoulders.

Getting there had been awful; getting back was far worse, even though they had the wind behind them. She slithered and stumbled along behind Jason's enormous back, thankful when he paused for a rest, clinging to his mac with numb hands. If she had had the breath she would have cheered when they reached the car. Instead she opened doors and laid out rugs and, when told to do so, got in beside Jimmy, who was reviving nicely, and held him steady while Jason took the car over the bridge once more, through the flooded village and finally home.

It was all rather a blur after that; it was only hours later, when Jason had driven away with Jimmy and his mother, bound for Odstock Hospital, that Araminta mulled over the day. Alone in the house, and uncertain when they would get back, she had tidied up, laid the table for a meal, put soup to simmer on the stove, fed the animals and made up the beds. Jason had told her to go to bed if they weren't back by eleven o'clock, but it was warm in the kitchen and the noise of the storm wasn't so loud. She put her head on the table and went to sleep.

When she woke it was one o'clock, and it seemed to her that the storm wasn't as fierce. She went upstairs and tumbled into bed, to wake to a thankfully quiet morning. The rain had stopped and the wind was a mere breeze. She crept downstairs and found Jason in the kitchen, making tea.

She blinked at him from a sleepy face. 'I went to bed. When did you get back? How is Jimmy?'

'Two o'clock and he's in his bed. His leg's in plaster and no harm done otherwise.'

She fetched mugs and milk and sugar and they sat together at the table and drank their tea. 'We'll go home today—after tea. Patty is spending a couple of days in Shaftesbury with friends—I'll fetch her later. Tom will be home this week, and I'll warn Dr Sloane.' He smiled from a tired face. 'Thank you, Araminta, I couldn't have managed without you!'

'I'll start getting breakfast,' said Araminta, not meeting his eye in case she said something she might regret later.

Their journey back wasn't easy; there were frequent halts where roads had been blocked, although on the main roads the floods were draining away already, so that it took twice as long as usual. Araminta heaved a great sigh of relief as they stopped in front of the house and Jason came to help her out. They hadn't talked much on the journey, but there had been no need. Now he said, 'I hope Mrs Buller has a meal ready.' He opened the front door and found Buller in the hall, hurrying to meet them.

'A very anxious time,' he observed. 'Me and Mrs Buller have been worried. There's some dinner ready when you would like it, ma'am.'

'Ten minutes? We're very hungry...'

'Perhaps you would like a tray in bed,' suggested the professor.

She looked astonished. 'Me? Oh, no, thank you, that is, unless...'

Jason was watching her, knowing what she was about to say. 'Good—may we have it in ten minutes or so, Buller?' And to Araminta he added, 'Time for a drink, my dear.'

All the same she went to bed early. There was a pile of letters by Jason's chair and a sheaf of messages he must be impatient to read. She wished him goodnight, expressed her pleasure at being home again, and went upstairs.

It was during the night that she woke and decided that something would have to be done. It wasn't honest to go on as they were; she would tell him that she had fallen in love with him and leave him to decide what to do. She had never been good at pretending... She went to sleep again, and when she woke it was morning. She remembered that he had a list, which meant that he would be up already.

She pulled on her dressing-gown, stuck her feet in slippers and flew downstairs. He was in the drawing-room, standing by the garden door while the dogs raced around on the little lawn. He had his post in one hand,

and as she went in he turned to look at her over his spectacles.

'Jason,' said Araminta. 'Jason—there's something I must tell you. Can you spare a minute?'

He put the letters down, took his spectacles off and put them in his pocket, and crossed the room. 'I can spare a whole lifetime for you, my own dear heart.'

She gave a great gulp, peering up at him through an untidy head of hair.

'You—what? I'm your own...?'

'Dear heart.' He nodded. 'Indeed you are, Araminta. I have been waiting for you all my life and when I found you I didn't know it—not at first.'

'Oh, Jason—you mean you love me too? I was going to tell you...'

He had taken her in his arms. 'Darling girl, a moment.' He bent to kiss her, gently at first and then with a fierce enjoyment which took her breath.

Perhaps there was no need to tell him, she thought dreamily, he seemed to know already. All the same she said firmly, 'I must tell you, my dear Jason, I love you too.' Then, when he had kissed her again, she added in a wifely voice, 'You'll be late for work, Jason.'

Buller, coming into the hall, heard the professor's shout of laughter and trod back to the kitchen. 'Happy ever after, that's what—didn't I tell you?' He beamed at his wife. 'Happy ever after and about time too!'

UNLOCK THE DOOR TO GREAT ROMANCE
AT BRIDE'S BAY RESORT

Join Harlequin's new across-the-lines series, set in an exclusive hotel on an island off the coast of South Carolina.

Seven of your favorite authors will bring you exciting stories about fascinating heroes and heroines discovering love at Bride's Bay Resort.

Look for these fabulous stories coming to a store near you beginning in January 1996.

Harlequin American Romance #613 in January
Matchmaking Baby by Cathy Gillen Thacker

Harlequin Presents #1794 in February
Indiscretions by Robyn Donald

Harlequin Intrigue #362 in March
Love and Lies by Dawn Stewardson

Harlequin Romance #3404 in April
Make Believe Engagement by Day Leclaire

Harlequin Temptation #588 in May
Stranger in the Night by Roseanne Williams

Harlequin Superromance #695 in June
Married to a Stranger by Connie Bennett

Harlequin Historicals #324 in July
Dulcie's Gift by Ruth Langan

Visit Bride's Bay Resort each month wherever
Harlequin books are sold.

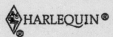

MILLION DOLLAR SWEEPSTAKES

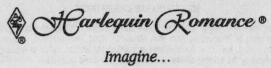

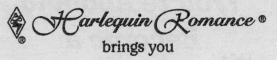

Harlequin Romance ®

brings you

How the West Was Wooed!

We've rounded up twelve of our most popular authors and the result is a whole year of romance, Western style. Every month we'll be bringing you a spirited, independent woman whose heart is about to be lassoed by a rugged, handsome, one-hundred-percent cowboy! Watch for...

You're About to Become a
Privileged
Woman

Reap the rewards of fabulous free gifts and
benefits with proofs-of-purchase from
Harlequin and Silhouette books

Pages & Privileges™

It's our way of thanking you for
buying our books at your
favorite retail stores.

**Harlequin and Silhouette—
the most privileged readers in the world!**

For more information about Harlequin and
Silhouette's PAGES & PRIVILEGES program call the
Pages & Privileges Benefits Desk: 1-503-794-2499

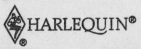

HARLEQUIN®

HR-PP159